ROD SERLING's THE TWILIGHT ZONE

THE BIG TALL WISH

Adaptation from Rod Serling's original script by

MARK KNEECE

Illustrated by

CHRIS LIE

WALKER & COMPANY
NEW YORK

INTRODUCTION

There is a fifth dimension beyond that which is known to man. It is a dimension as vast as space and timeless as infinity. It is the middle ground between light and shadow, between science and superstition, and it lies between the pit of man's fears and the summit of his knowledge. This is the dimension of imagination. It is an area which we call the Twilight Zone.

America, between the 1950s and early 1960s, was itself in a sort of "twilight zone." Following the victories of World War II and the attending economic boom—but before the Civil Rights marches; the assassinations of John F. Kennedy, Martin Luther King, Jr., and Robert F. Kennedy; and the Vietnam War—we were wrapped in a gleaming package of shining chrome, white picket fences, and Hollywood glamour. But beneath this shimmering facade lay a turbulent core of racial inequality, sexual inequality, and the Cold War threat of nuclear attacks from the Soviet Union. We'd never been more affluent—or more frightened.

Enter Rodman Edward Serling of Binghamton, New York. Serling began writing in his teens for his high school newspaper; as a student at Antioch College, he was already selling scripts to radio programs. While serving as a paratrooper in the U.S. Army Eleventh Airborne (for which he earned a Purple Heart), he wrote for the Armed Services Radio. He went on to write for film and television, first in feature presentations for *Hallmark Hall of Fame* and *Playhouse 90*, including the lauded "Requiem for a Heavyweight," perhaps drawing inspiration from his own experiences as a Golden Gloves boxer. More than two hundred of his teleplays were produced. In all, his work would win not only the adoration of listeners and viewers but a host of prestigious awards, including a record-breaking six Emmy awards—two of them for his greatest achievement, *The Twilight Zone*.

The worlds and characters presented over the course of five seasons, beginning in October 1959, were like nothing audiences had seen before. Television, the new "must have" appliance for America's increasingly prosperous households, offered comedies such as *I Love Lucy* and *The Honeymooners*, news programs including Edward R. Murrow's *See It Now*, as well as Westerns, game shows, and soap operas. With a typewriter as his spade, Serling dug beneath the surface of the expected and planted the seeds of a more imaginative and thoughtful genre, writing more than half of the show's 156 episodes while producing and hosting all of them. He bravely took on themes of oppression, prejudice, and paranoia, all the while giving people what they needed at the end of the day: entertainment.

While he had his run-ins with censorship, Serling's clever use of other worlds and veiled scenarios generally protected him. As he explained, what he couldn't have a Republican or a Democrat espouse on the show, he could have an alien profess without offending the sponsors. This approach also allowed viewers to take away whatever message best suited them; the more reflective could consider the psychological and political implications, while others might be satisfied with simply enjoying the thrill of the surface story. So much more than mere science fiction or fantasy, Serling's scripts are parables that explore the multifaceted natures of hope, fear, humanity, loneliness, and self-delusion.

Half a century later, *The Twilight Zone* remains a part of our culture, routinely referenced in print and on television, having become a shorthand expression that succinctly describes the bizarre and unexpected. The original episodes are still aired on the SciFi Channel, both in late-night slots and as day-long marathons. The show was literally a Who's Who of Hollywood, helping to foster the careers of fledgling actors including Robert Redford, Ron Howard, Dennis Hopper, Charles Bronson, and William Shatner. It has also inspired countless authors and filmmakers, who have gone on to break through boundaries of their own.

In the fifty years since *The Twilight Zone* first aired, we've faced new enemies and have altered our definitions of happiness, but our core hopes and fears remain the same, as does our desire to be entertained. The stories are as compelling, and as telling, as ever. And now, in their newest incarnation, Serling's scripts serve as the basis for this graphic novel series, which honors the original text and even echoes the storyboarding of television, but offers a fresh interpretation, as seen through the eyes of a new generation of artists.

—Anna Marlis Burgard
Director of Industry Partnerships, Savannah College of Art and Design

You're traveling through
another dimension,
a dimension not only of sight and sound
but of mind;
a journey into a wondrous land
whose boundaries
are that of imagination.
That's the signpost up ahead—
your next stop,
the Twilight Zone!

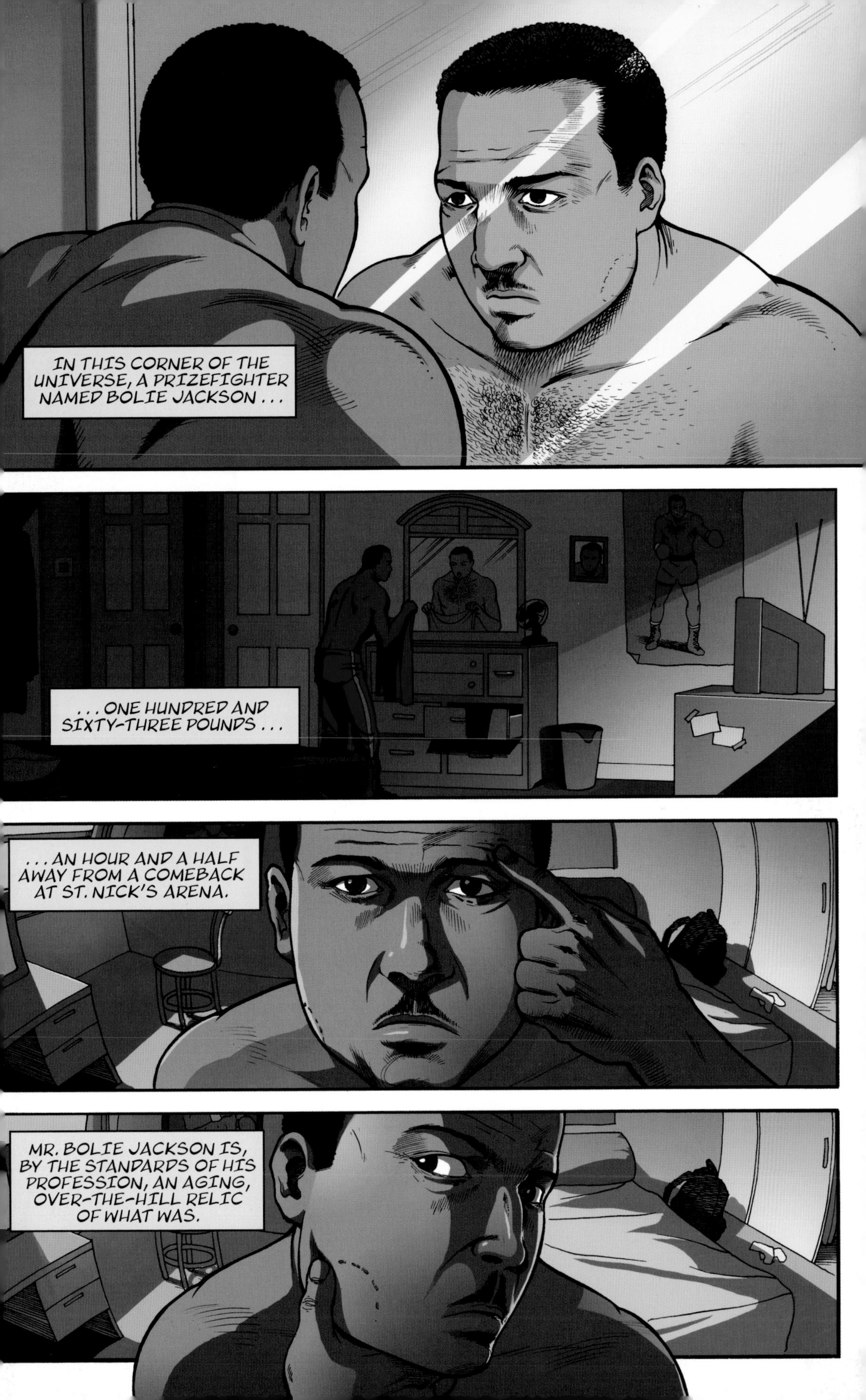
IN THIS CORNER OF THE UNIVERSE, A PRIZEFIGHTER NAMED BOLIE JACKSON . . .
. . . ONE HUNDRED AND SIXTY-THREE POUNDS . . .
. . . AN HOUR AND A HALF AWAY FROM A COMEBACK AT ST. NICK'S ARENA.
MR. BOLIE JACKSON IS, BY THE STANDARDS OF HIS PROFESSION, AN AGING, OVER-THE-HILL RELIC OF WHAT WAS.

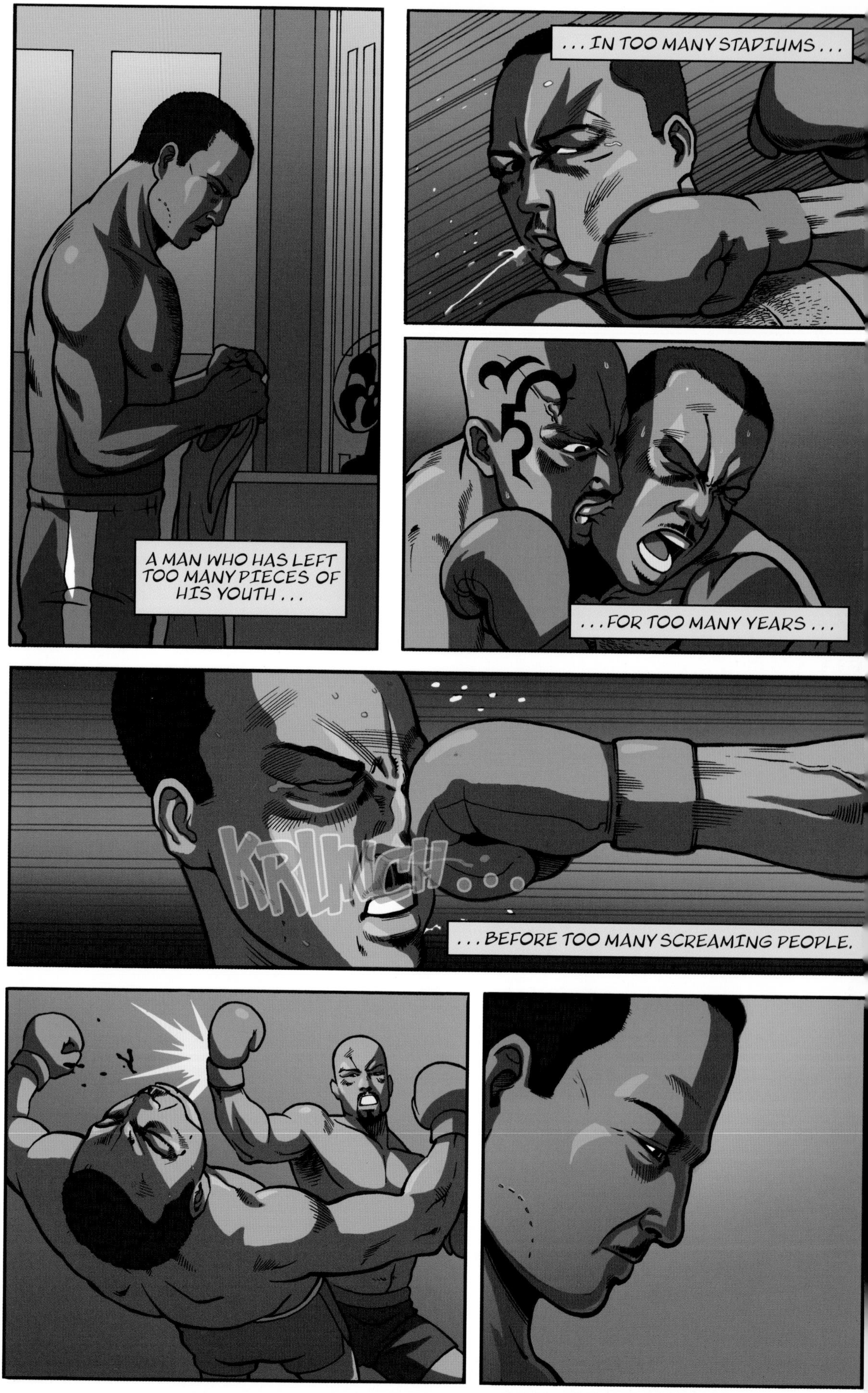
A MAN WHO HAS LEFT TOO MANY PIECES OF HIS YOUTH . . .
. . . IN TOO MANY STADIUMS . . .
. . . FOR TOO MANY YEARS . . .
KRUNCH
. . . BEFORE TOO MANY SCREAMING PEOPLE.

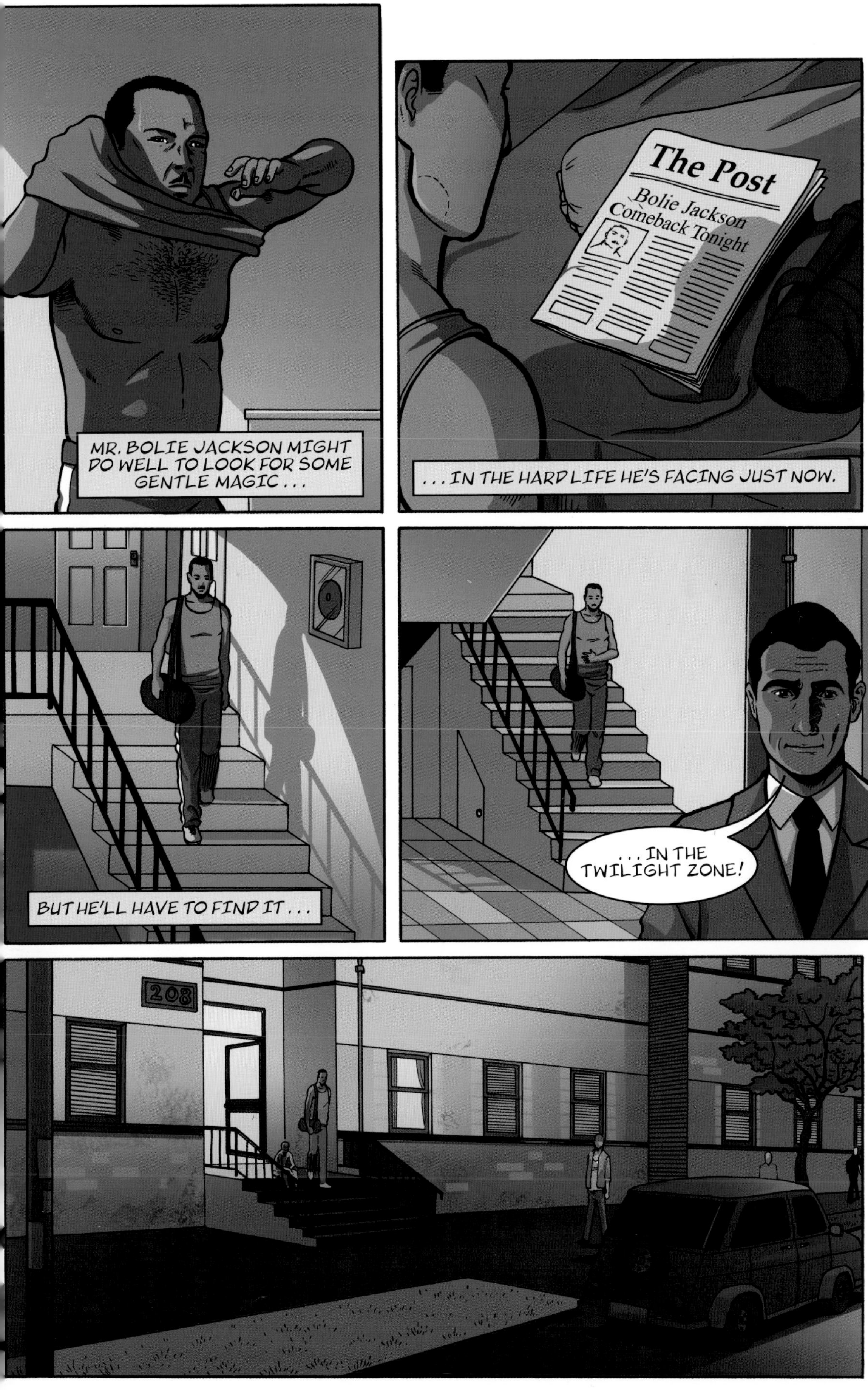
MR. BOLIE JACKSON MIGHT DO WELL TO LOOK FOR SOME GENTLE MAGIC . . .
The Post
Bolie Jackson Comeback Tonight
. . . IN THE HARD LIFE HE'S FACING JUST NOW.
BUT HE'LL HAVE TO FIND IT . . .
. . . IN THE TWILIGHT ZONE!
208

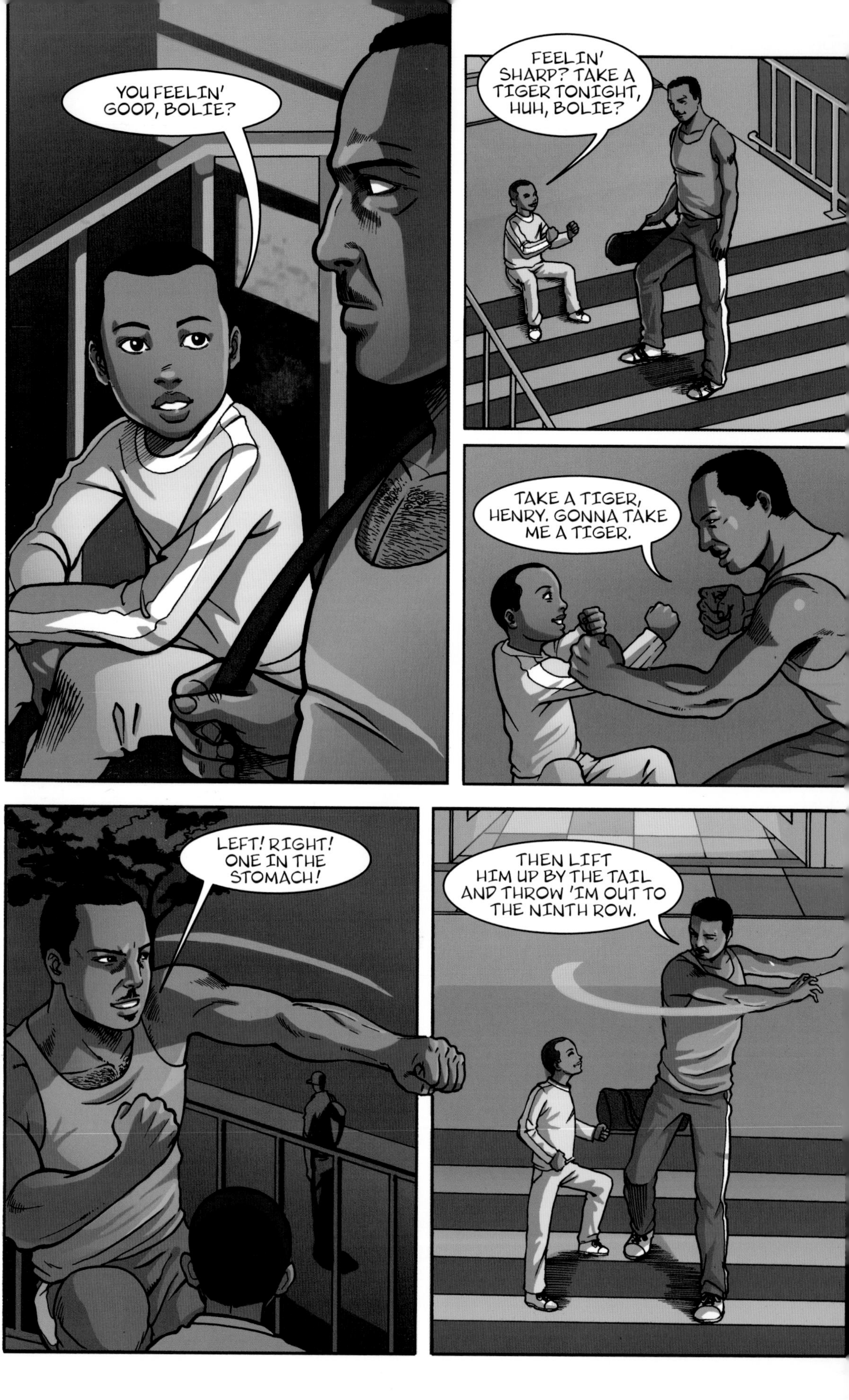
YOU FEELIN' GOOD, BOLIE?
FEELIN' SHARP? TAKE A TIGER TONIGHT, HUH, BOLIE?
TAKE A TIGER, HENRY. GONNA TAKE ME A TIGER.
LEFT! RIGHT! ONE IN THE STOMACH!
THEN LIFT HIM UP BY THE TAIL AND THROW 'IM OUT TO THE NINTH ROW.

YOU'RE LOOKIN' GOOD, BOLIE! LOOKIN' SHARP, MAN.

YOU GONNA WATCH THE FIGHT?

YOU FOOLIN'? I'LL YELL SO LOUD YOU'LL HEAR ME ALL THE WAY TO ST. NICK'S.

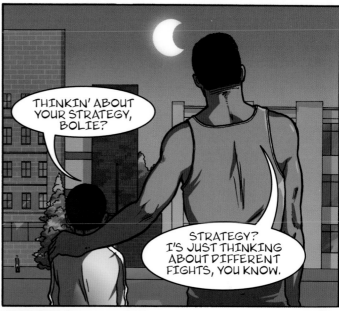

THINKIN' ABOUT YOUR STRATEGY, BOLIE?

STRATEGY? I'S JUST THINKING ABOUT DIFFERENT FIGHTS, YOU KNOW.

AND A FIGHTER DON'T NEED A SCRAPBOOK.

KNOW HOW TO TELL WHAT A FIGHTER'S DONE? WHERE HE'S FOUGHT?

THE WHOLE STORY'S RIGHT THERE ON HIS FACE LIKE A ROAD MAP.

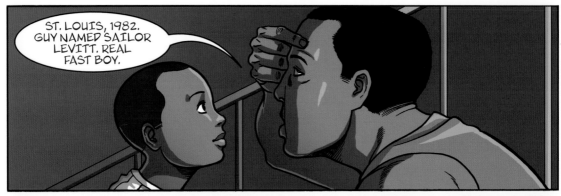

ST. LOUIS, 1982. GUY NAMED SAILOR LEVITT. REAL FAST BOY.

THAT WAS MEMORIAL STADIUM, SYRACUSE, NEW YORK. ITALIAN BOY, FOUGHT LIKE MARCIANO.

ALL HANDS AND ARMS LIKE A WINDMILL ALL OVER YOU. FIRST TIME I EVER HAD MY NOSE BROKEN TWICE IN ONE FIGHT.

MIAMI, FLORIDA. BOY GOT ME UP AGAINST A RING POST.

RIPPED ME UP WITH HIS LACES.

ON THE FACE, HENRY, THAT'S WHERE YOU READ IT— ALL THE FIGHTS, ALL THE THINGS HE ALMOST HAD BUT NEVER GOT. . . .

START IN 1972, THEN MOVE ACROSS . . . PITTSBURGH, BOSTON, SYRACUSE . . .

TIRED OLD MAN, HENRY. TIRED OLD MAN . . .

. . . TRYIN' TO CATCH A BUS.

COME ON, MAN . . . YOU THINK YOU GOT IT?! SHOW ME SOMETHING!

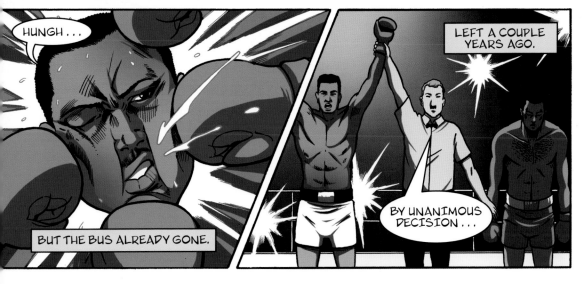

HUNGH . . .

BUT THE BUS ALREADY GONE.

LEFT A COUPLE YEARS AGO.

BY UNANIMOUS DECISION . . .

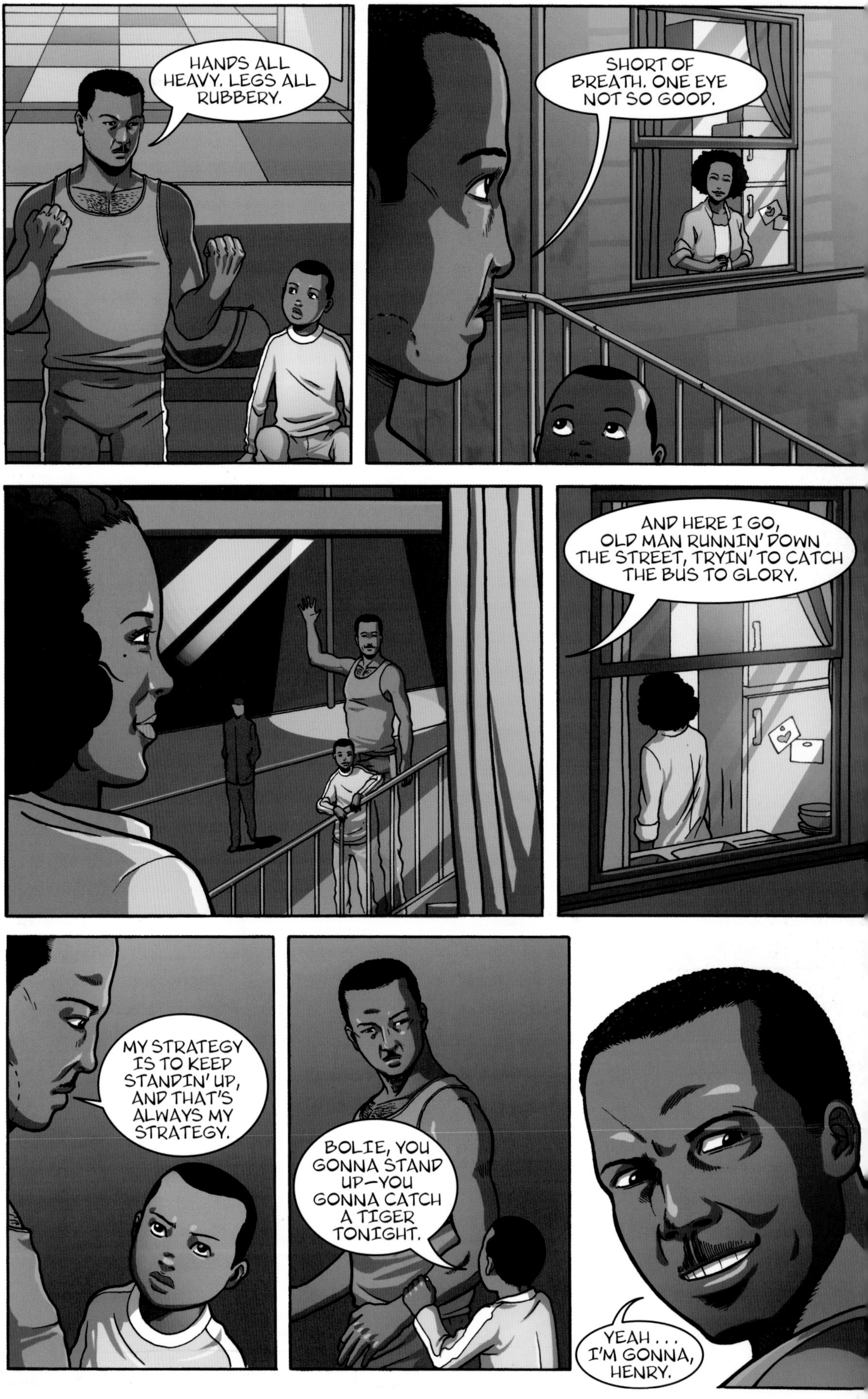
HANDS ALL HEAVY. LEGS ALL RUBBERY.
SHORT OF BREATH. ONE EYE NOT SO GOOD.
AND HERE I GO, OLD MAN RUNNIN' DOWN THE STREET, TRYIN' TO CATCH THE BUS TO GLORY.
MY STRATEGY IS TO KEEP STANDIN' UP, AND THAT'S ALWAYS MY STRATEGY.
BOLIE, YOU GONNA STAND UP—YOU GONNA CATCH A TIGER TONIGHT.
YEAH . . . I'M GONNA, HENRY.

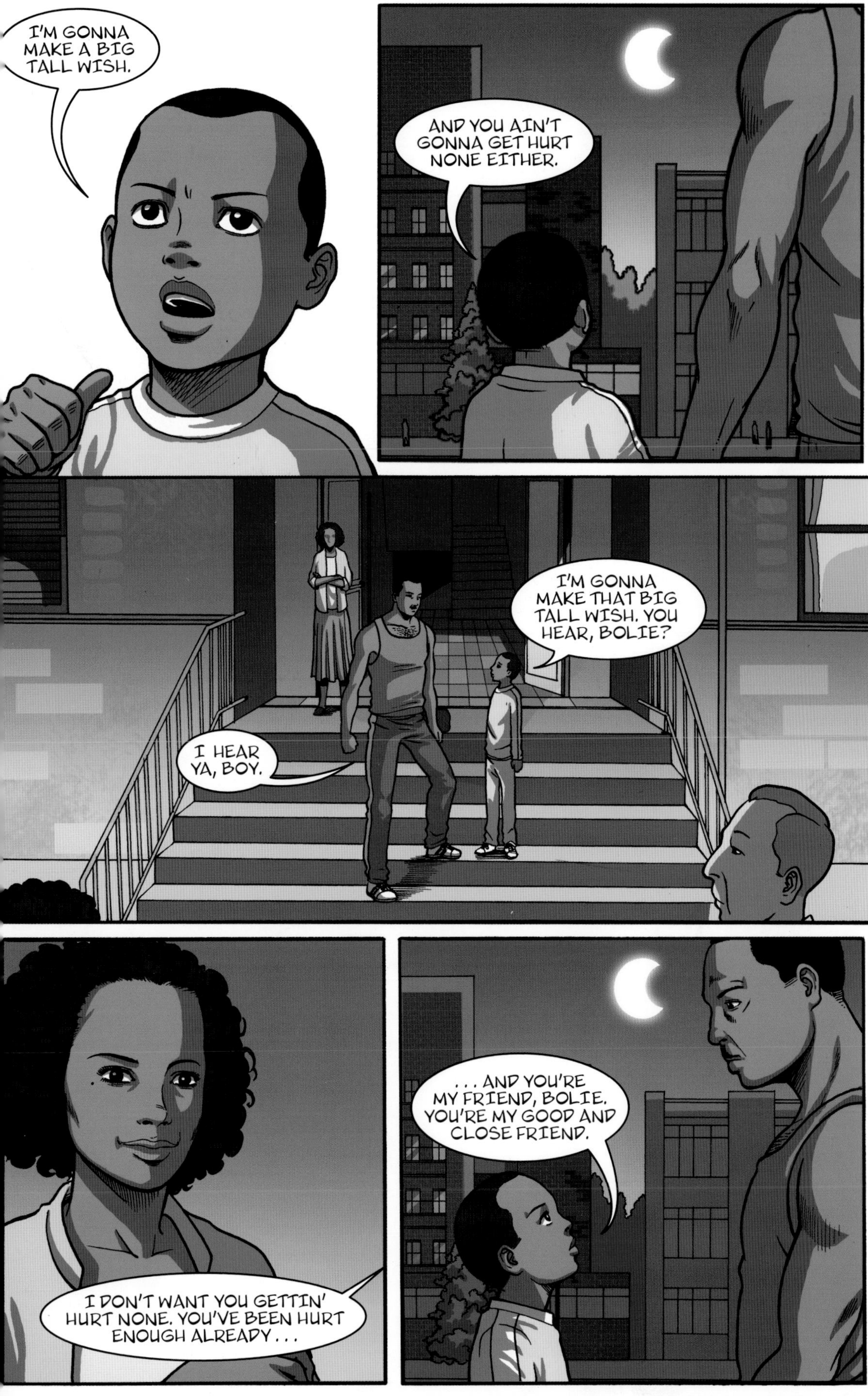
I'M GONNA MAKE A BIG TALL WISH.
AND YOU AIN'T GONNA GET HURT NONE EITHER.
I'M GONNA MAKE THAT BIG TALL WISH. YOU HEAR, BOLIE?
I HEAR YA, BOY.
I DON'T WANT YOU GETTIN' HURT NONE. YOU'VE BEEN HURT ENOUGH ALREADY . . .
. . . AND YOU'RE MY FRIEND, BOLIE. YOU'RE MY GOOD AND CLOSE FRIEND.

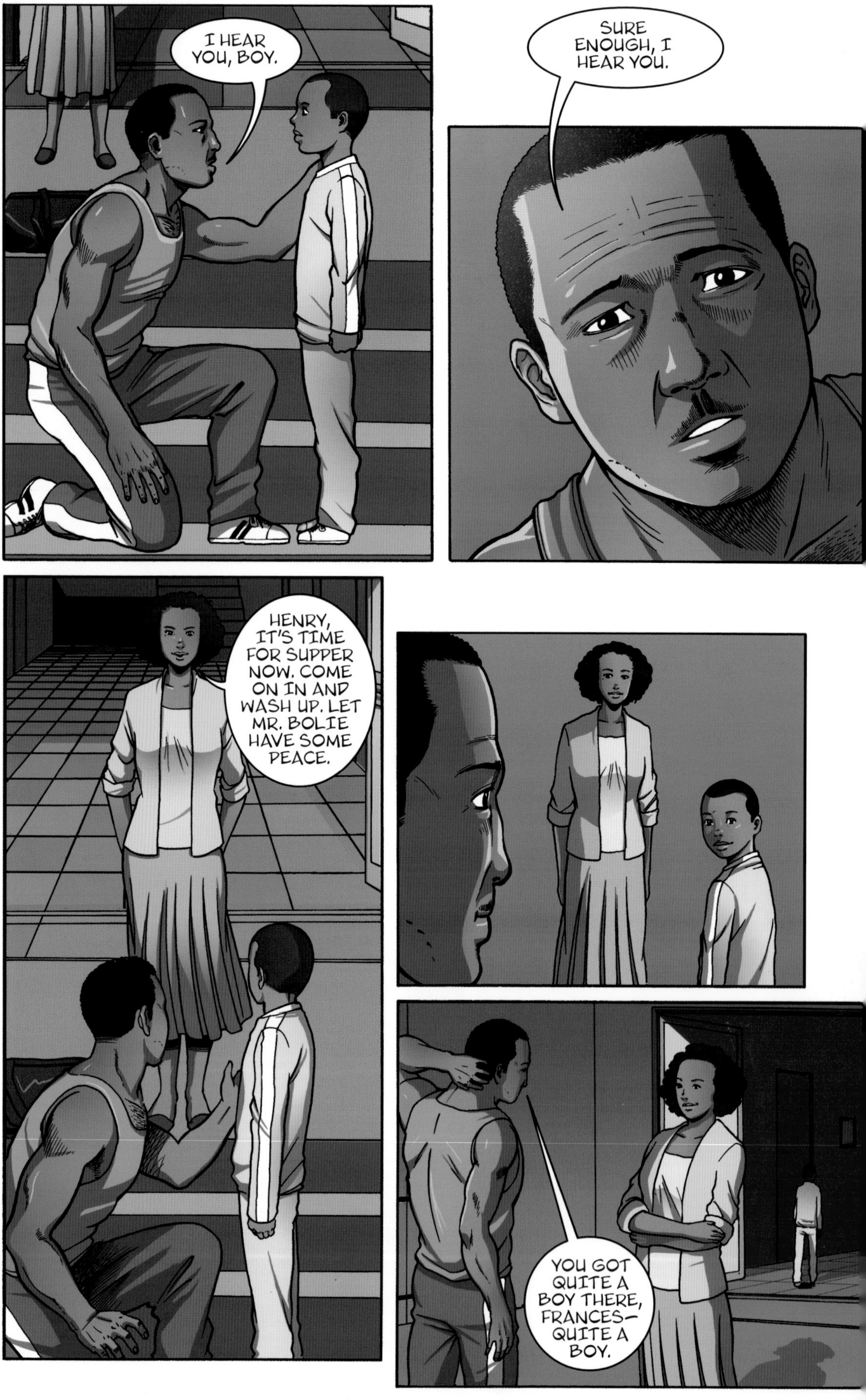
I HEAR YOU, BOY.
SURE ENOUGH, I HEAR YOU.
HENRY, IT'S TIME FOR SUPPER NOW. COME ON IN AND WASH UP. LET MR. BOLIE HAVE SOME PEACE.
YOU GOT QUITE A BOY THERE, FRANCES— QUITE A BOY.

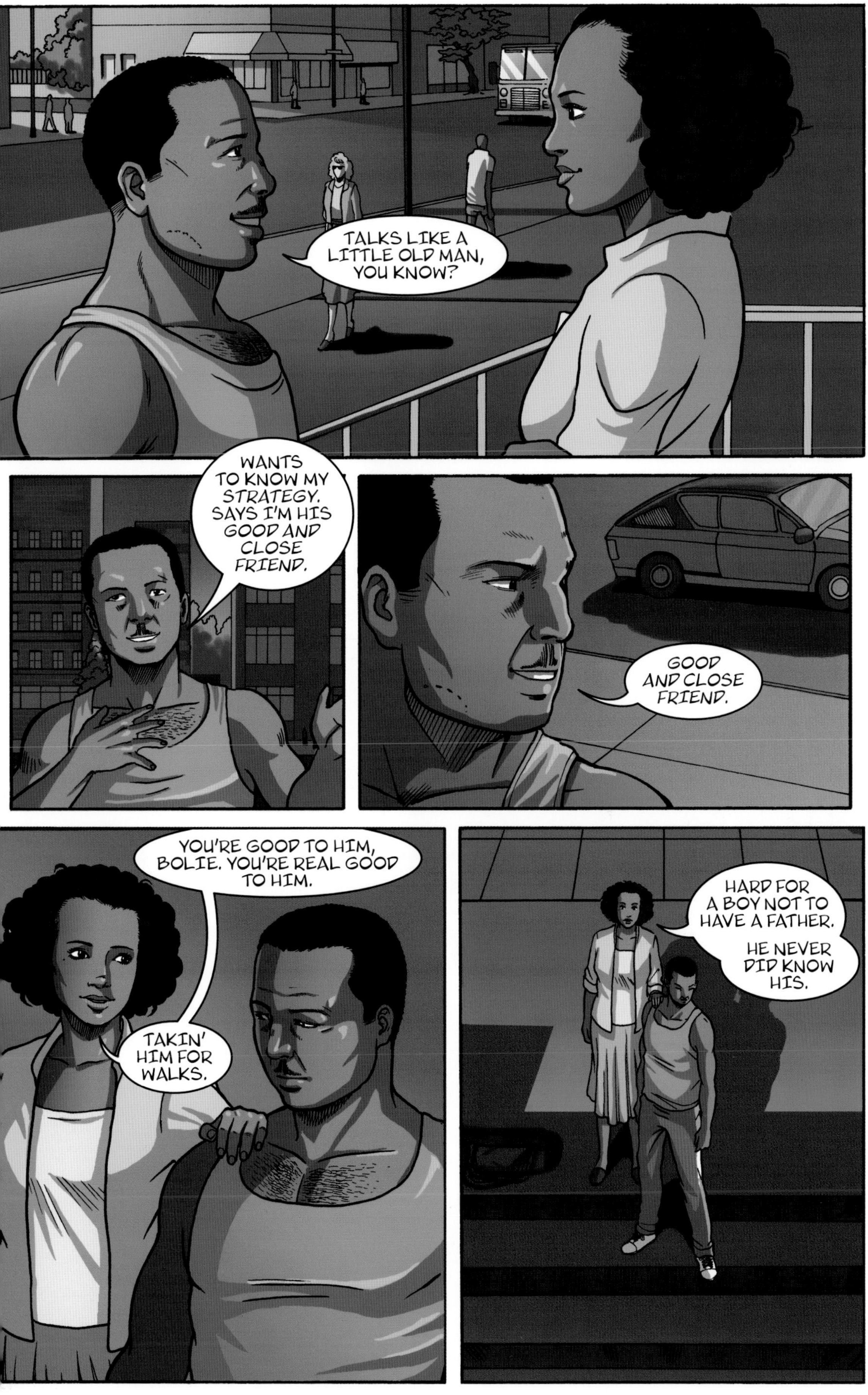
TALKS LIKE A LITTLE OLD MAN, YOU KNOW?
WANTS TO KNOW MY STRATEGY. SAYS I'M HIS GOOD AND CLOSE FRIEND.
GOOD AND CLOSE FRIEND.
YOU'RE GOOD TO HIM, BOLIE. YOU'RE REAL GOOD TO HIM.
TAKIN' HIM FOR WALKS.
HARD FOR A BOY NOT TO HAVE A FATHER.
HE NEVER DID KNOW HIS.

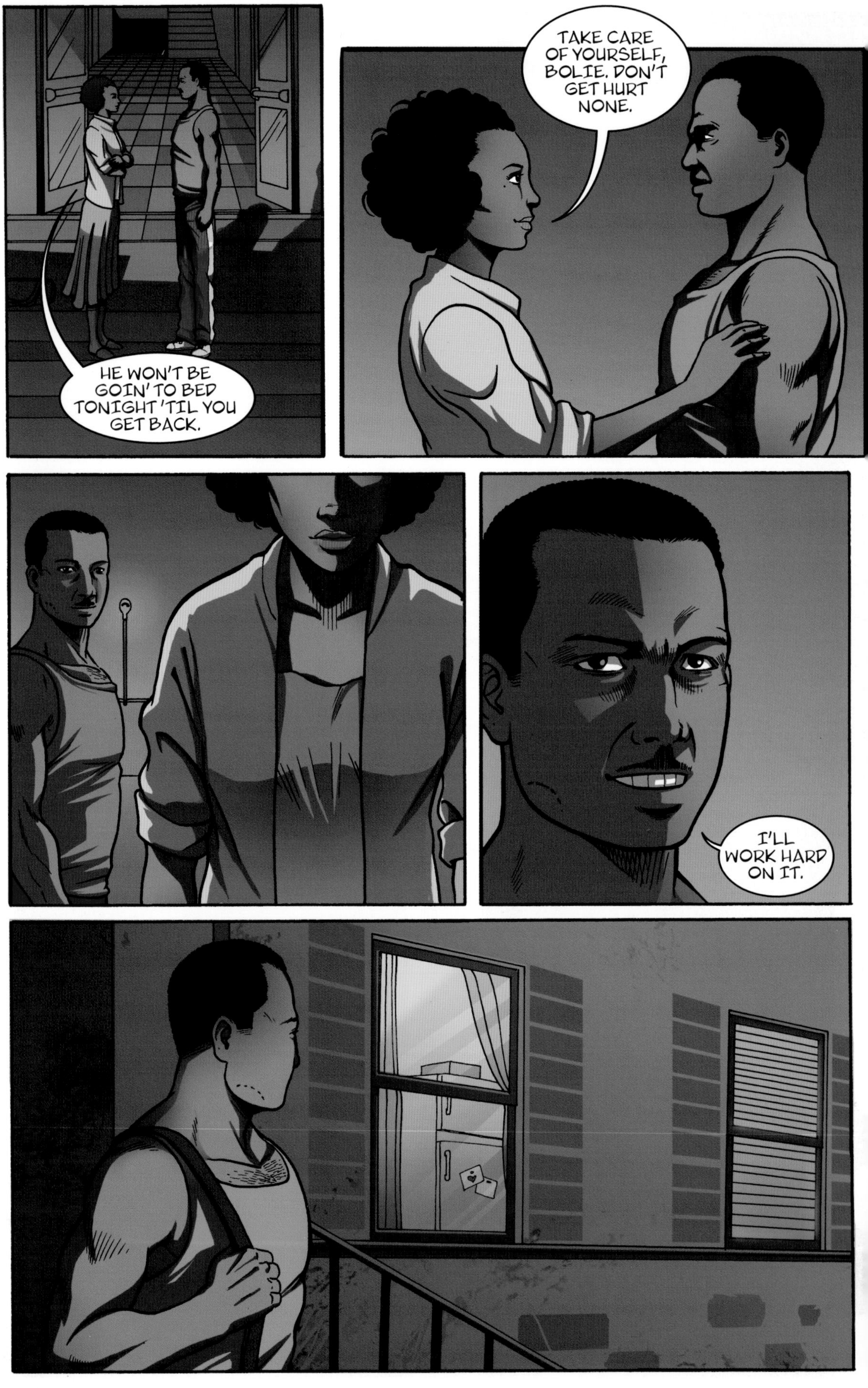
HE WON'T BE GOIN' TO BED TONIGHT 'TIL YOU GET BACK.
TAKE CARE OF YOURSELF, BOLIE. DON'T GET HURT NONE.
I'LL WORK HARD ON IT.

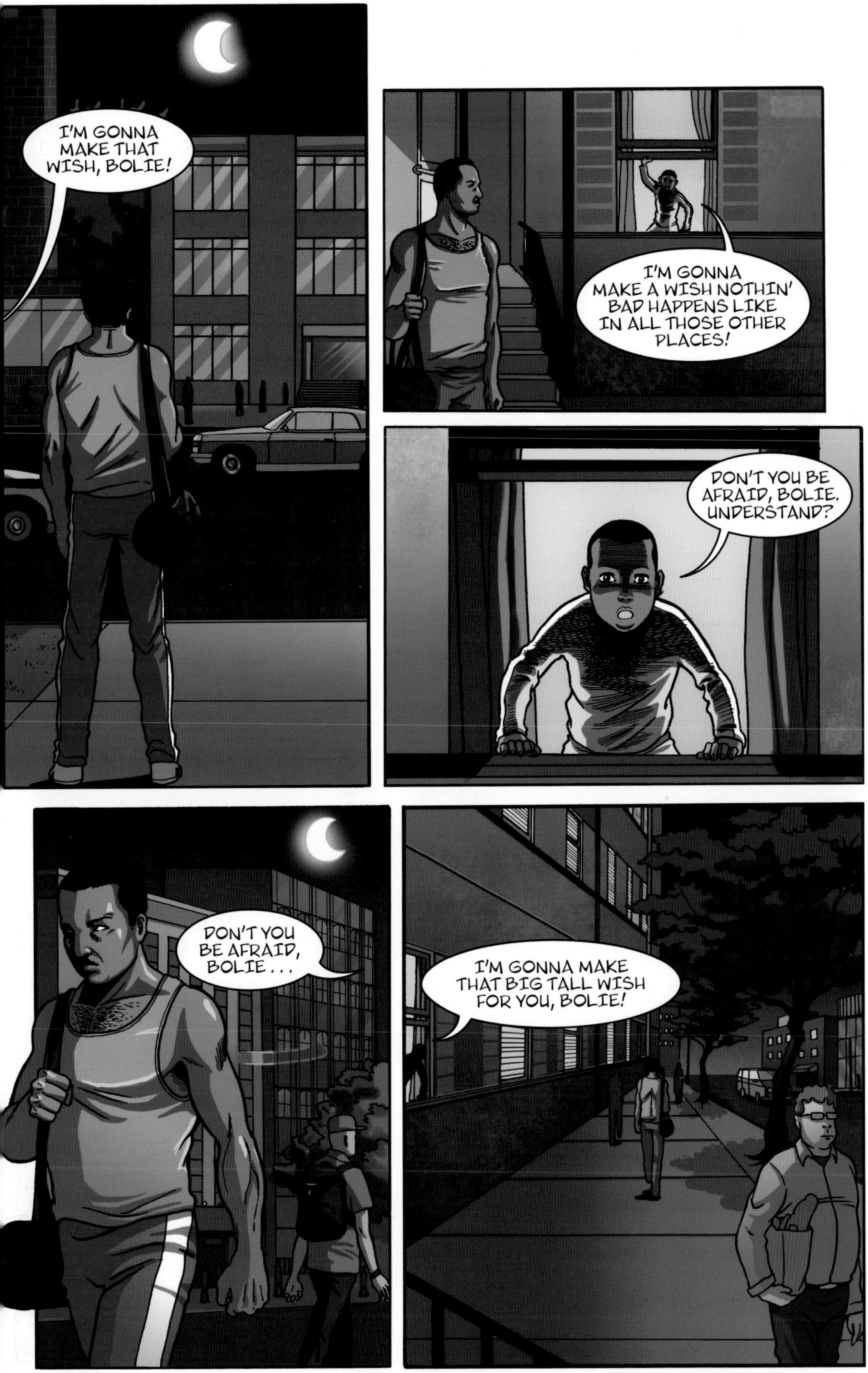
I'M GONNA MAKE THAT WISH, BOLIE!
I'M GONNA MAKE A WISH NOTHIN' BAD HAPPENS LIKE IN ALL THOSE OTHER PLACES!
DON'T YOU BE AFRAID, BOLIE. UNDERSTAND?
DON'T YOU BE AFRAID, BOLIE . . .
I'M GONNA MAKE THAT BIG TALL WISH FOR YOU, BOLIE!

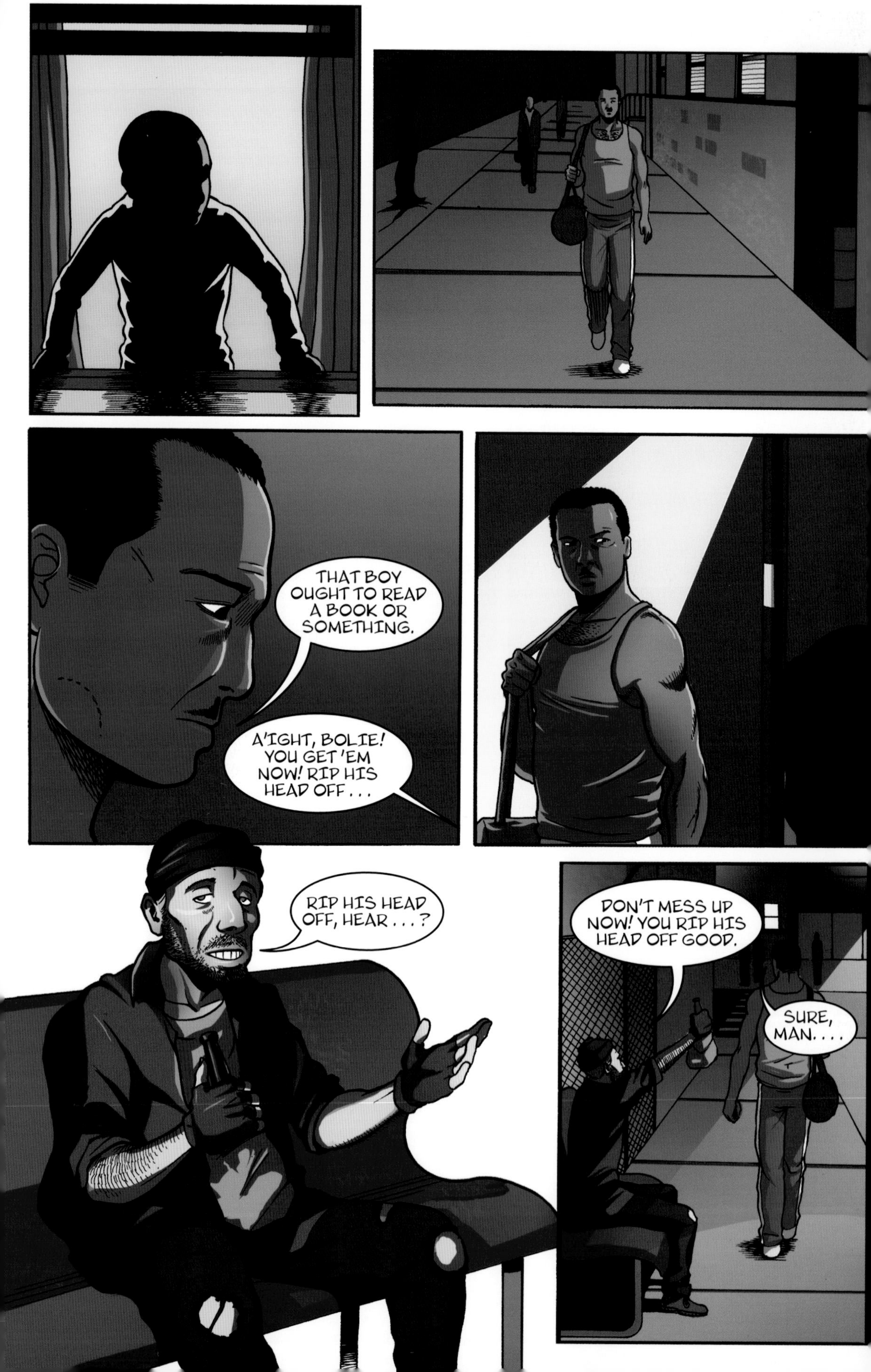
THAT BOY OUGHT TO READ A BOOK OR SOMETHING.
A'IGHT, BOLIE! YOU GET 'EM NOW! RIP HIS HEAD OFF . . .
RIP HIS HEAD OFF, HEAR . . . ?
DON'T MESS UP NOW! YOU RIP HIS HEAD OFF GOOD.
SURE, MAN. . . .

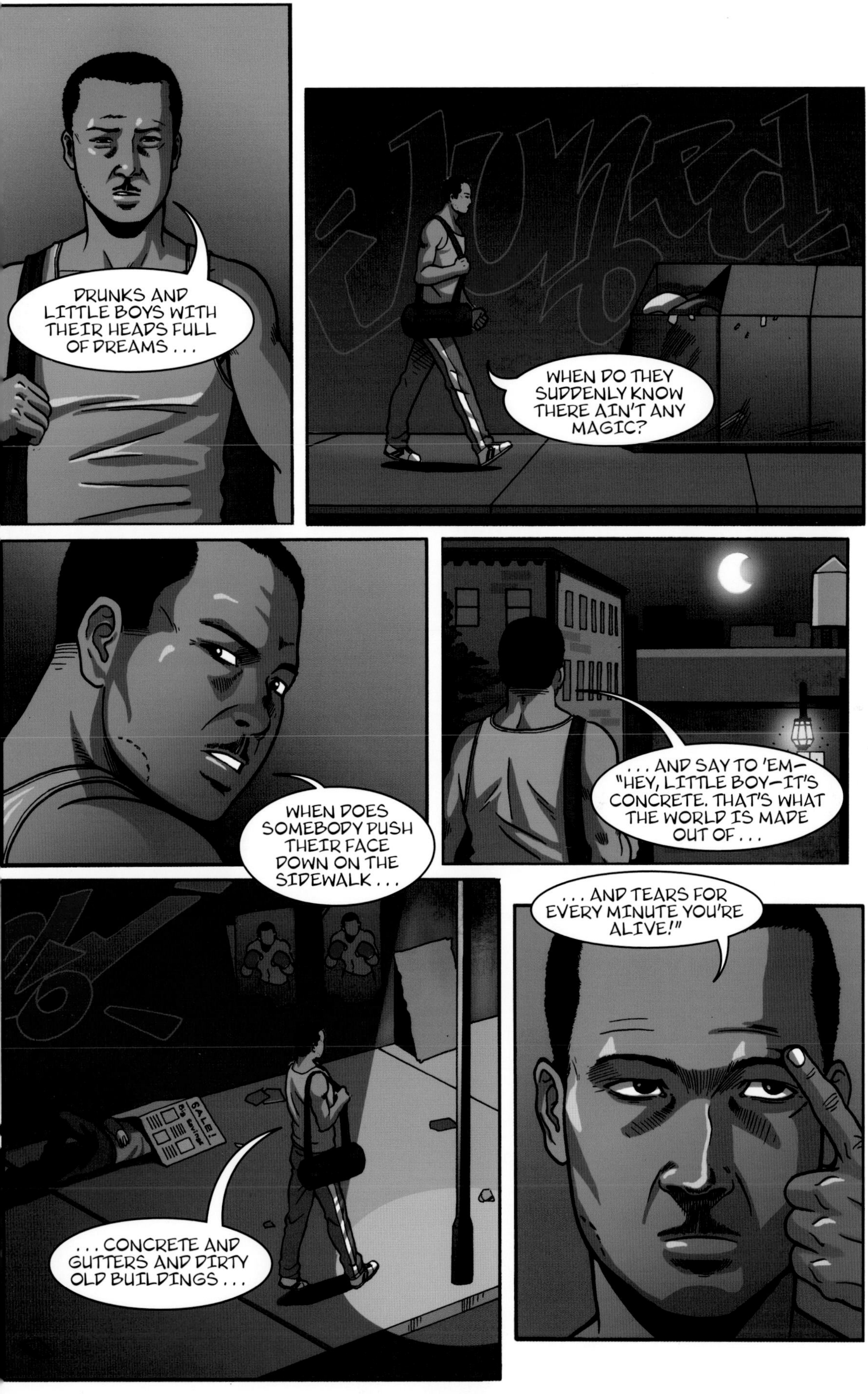
DRUNKS AND LITTLE BOYS WITH THEIR HEADS FULL OF DREAMS . . .
WHEN DO THEY SUDDENLY KNOW THERE AIN'T ANY MAGIC?
WHEN DOES SOMEBODY PUSH THEIR FACE DOWN ON THE SIDEWALK . . .
. . . AND SAY TO 'EM— "HEY, LITTLE BOY—IT'S CONCRETE. THAT'S WHAT THE WORLD IS MADE OUT OF . . .
. . . CONCRETE AND GUTTERS AND DIRTY OLD BUILDINGS . . .
. . . AND TEARS FOR EVERY MINUTE YOU'RE ALIVE!"

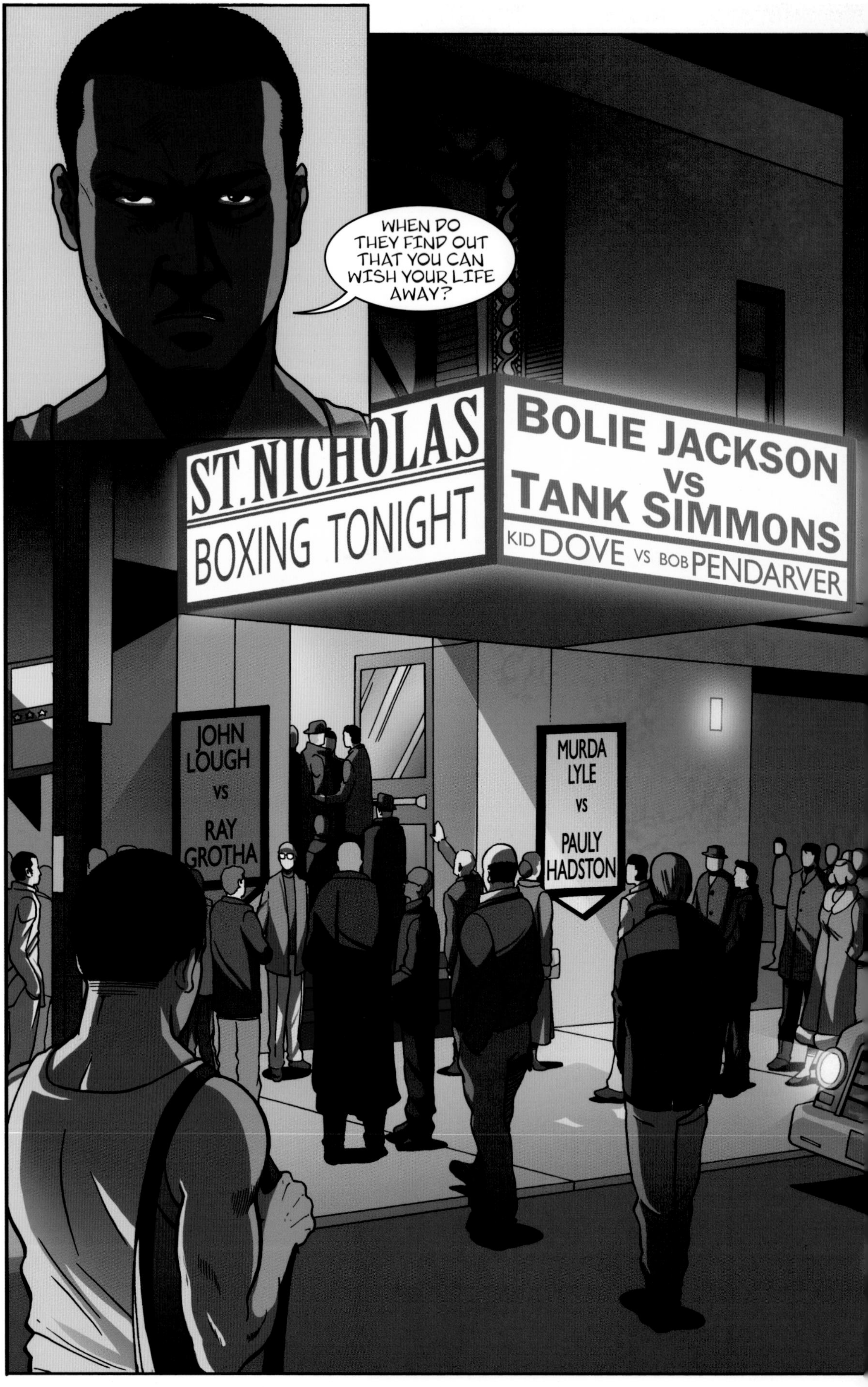
WHEN DO THEY FIND OUT THAT YOU CAN WISH YOUR LIFE AWAY?
ST. NICHOLAS
BOXING TONIGHT
BOLIE JACKSON VS TANK SIMMONS
KID DOVE VS BOB PENDARVER
JOHN LOUGH VS RAY GROTHA
MURDA LYLE VS PAULY HADSTON

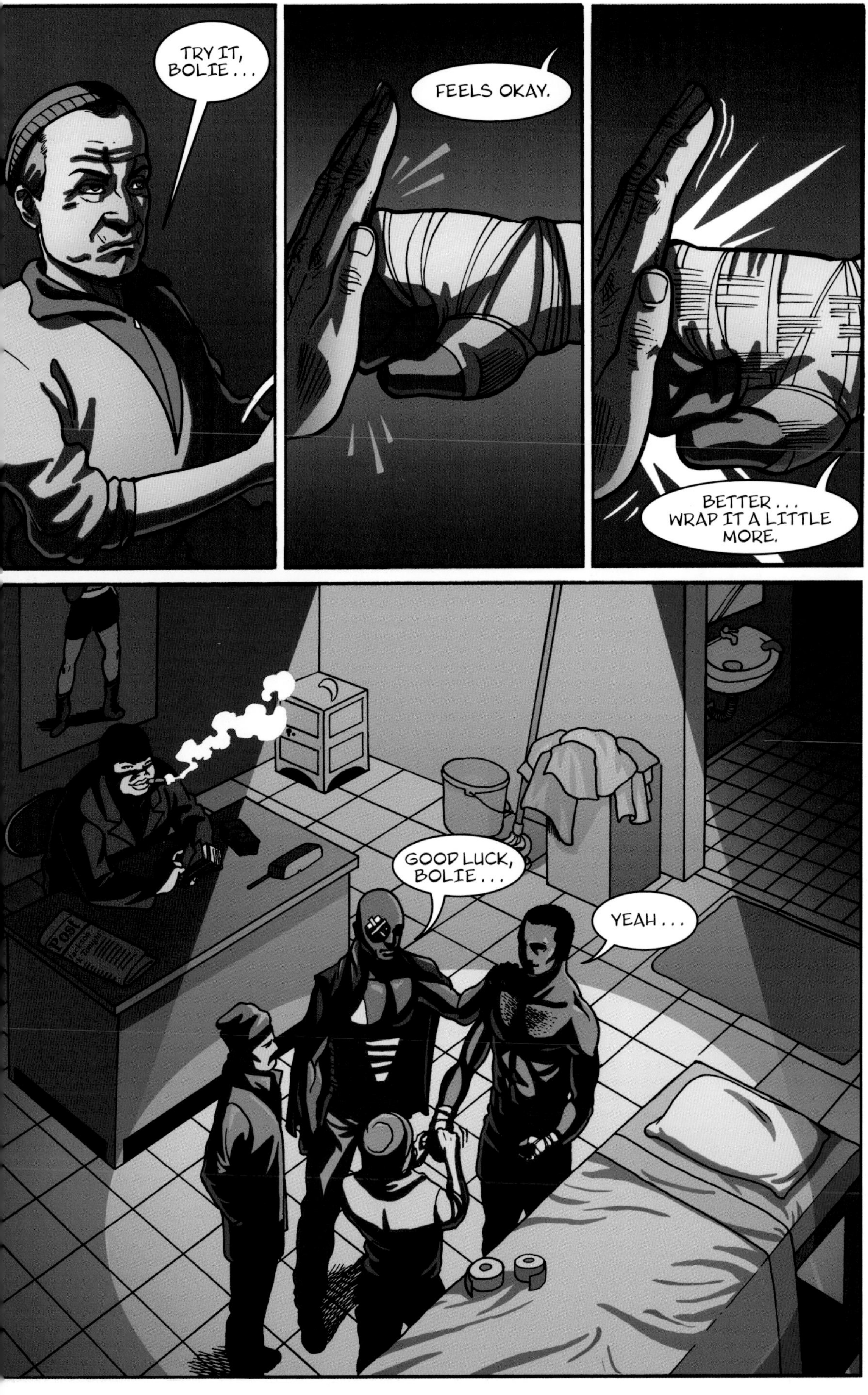
TRY IT, BOLIE . . .
FEELS OKAY.
BETTER . . . WRAP IT A LITTLE MORE.
GOOD LUCK, BOLIE . . .
YEAH . . .

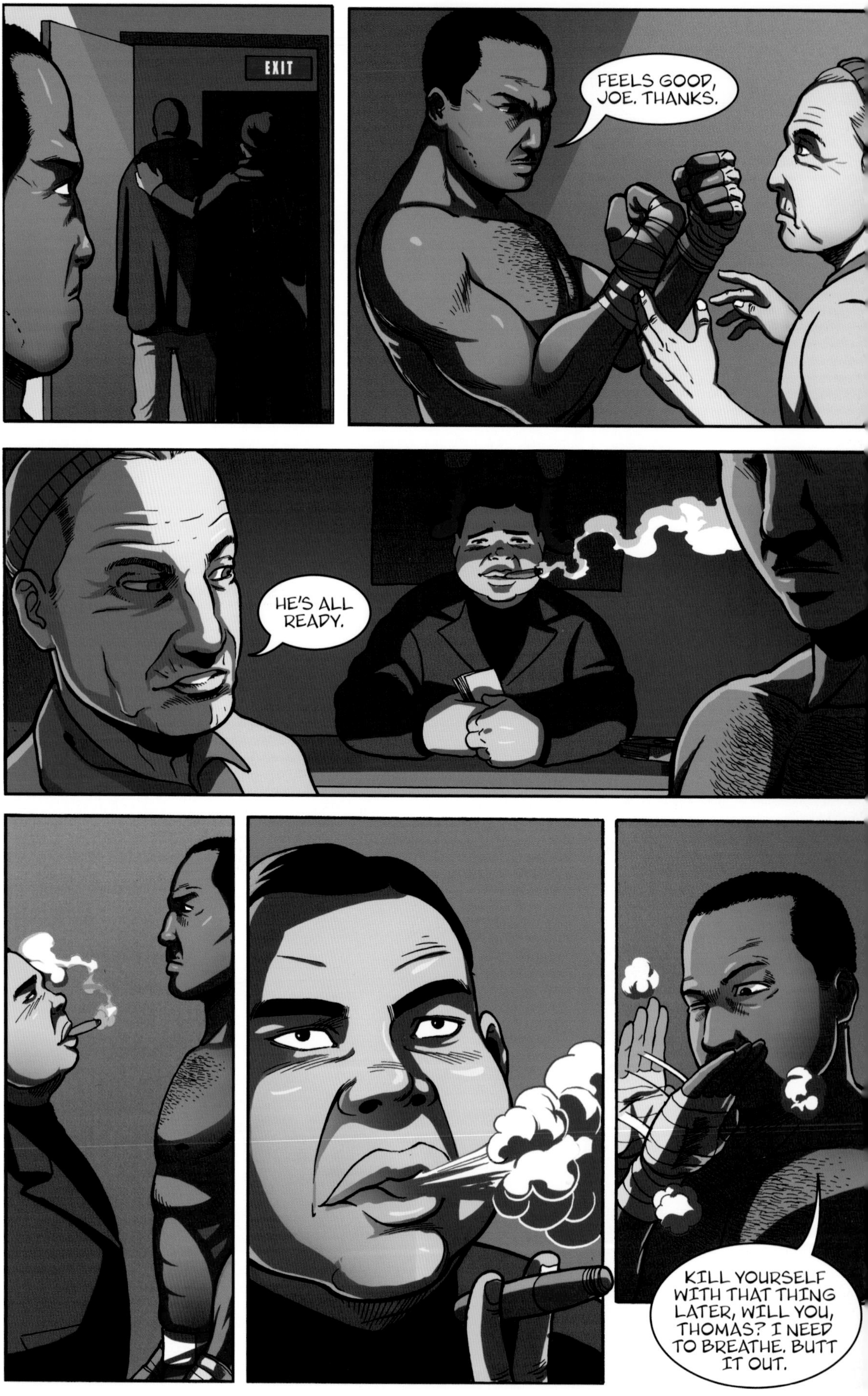
EXIT
FEELS GOOD, JOE. THANKS.
HE'S ALL READY.
KILL YOURSELF WITH THAT THING LATER, WILL YOU, THOMAS? I NEED TO BREATHE. BUTT IT OUT.

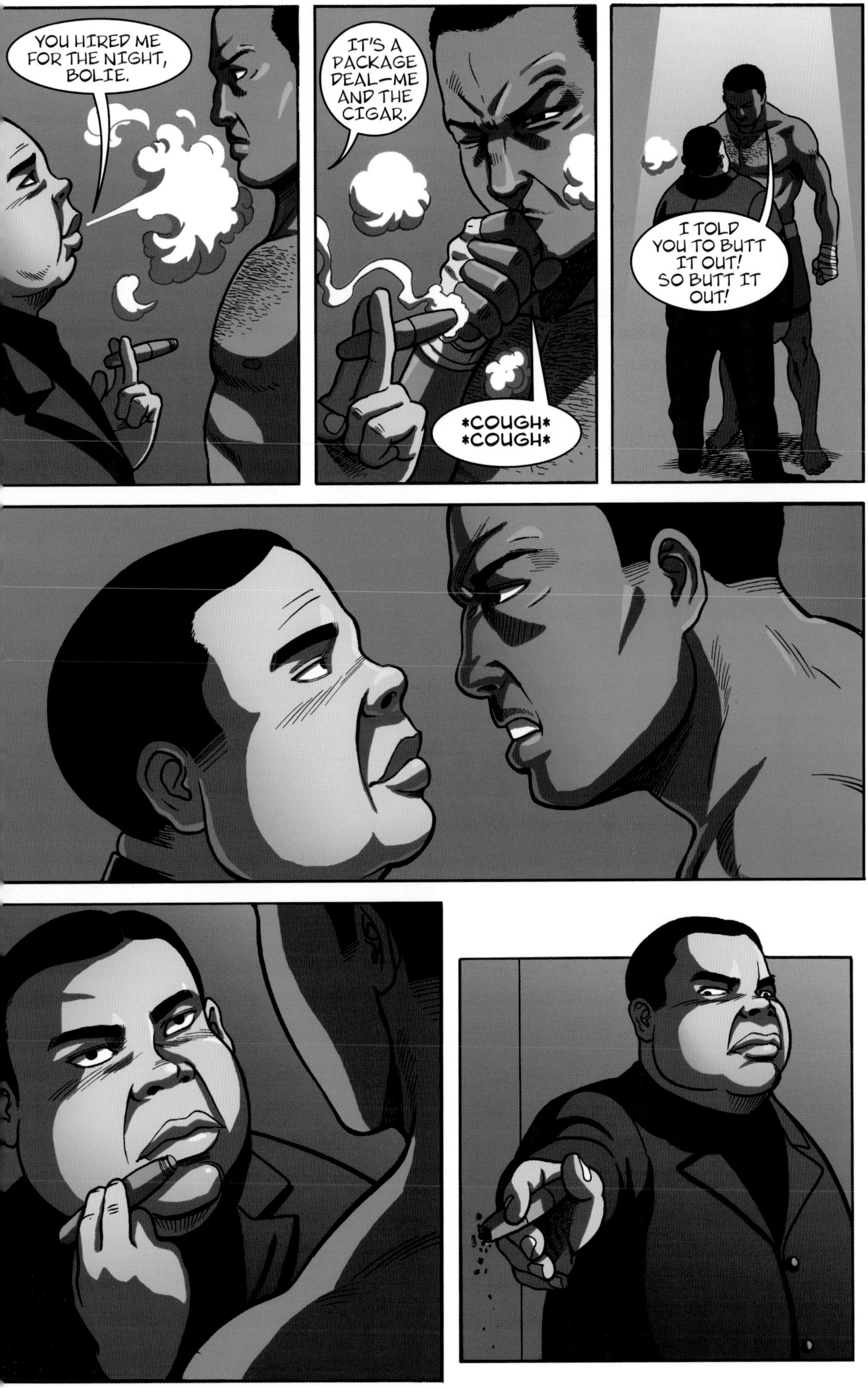
YOU HIRED ME FOR THE NIGHT, BOLIE.
IT'S A PACKAGE DEAL—ME AND THE CIGAR.
COUGH *COUGH*
I TOLD YOU TO BUTT IT OUT! SO BUTT IT OUT!

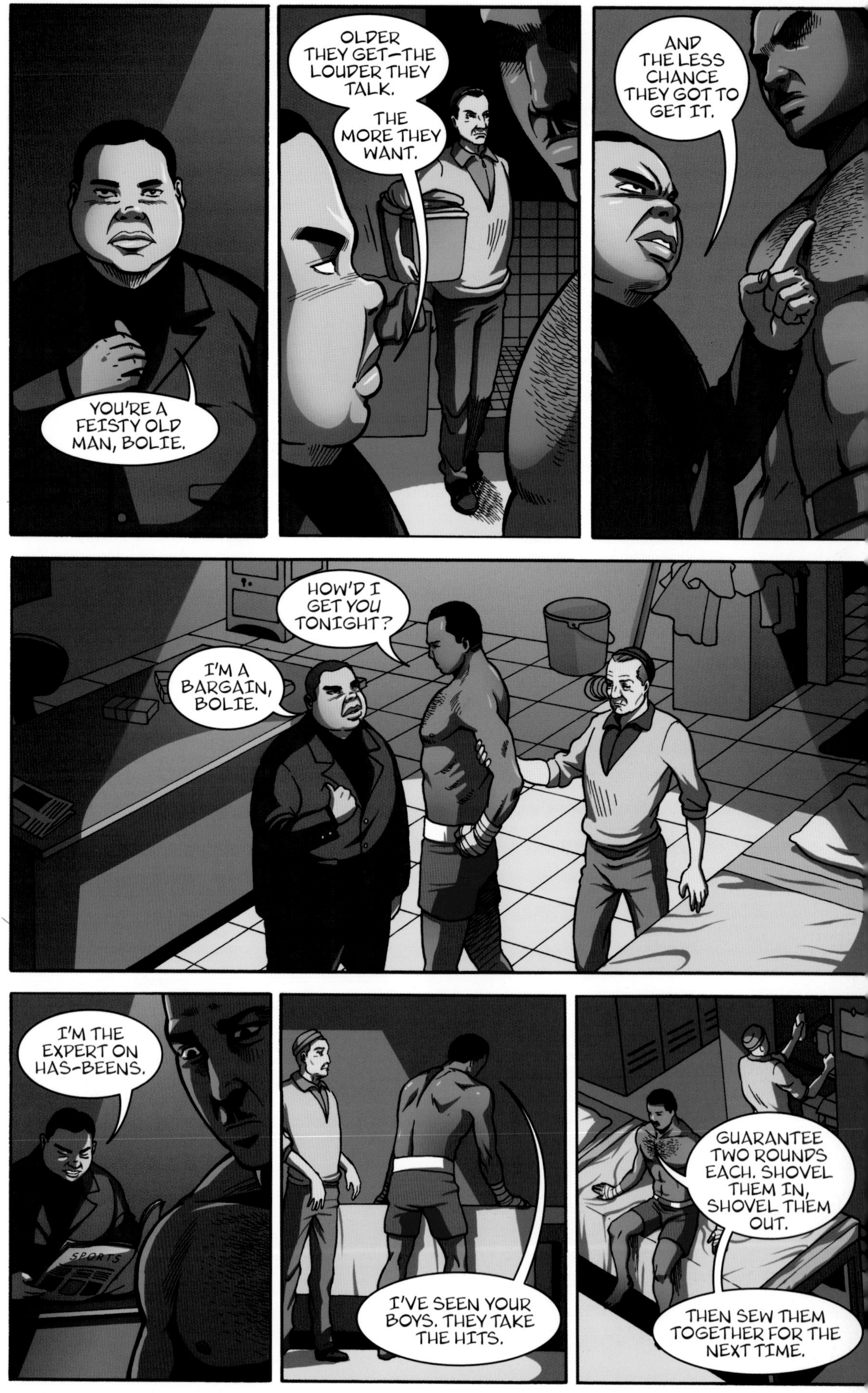
YOU'RE A FEISTY OLD MAN, BOLIE.
OLDER THEY GET—THE LOUDER THEY TALK.
THE MORE THEY WANT.
AND THE LESS CHANCE THEY GOT TO GET IT.
HOW'D I GET YOU TONIGHT?
I'M A BARGAIN, BOLIE.
I'M THE EXPERT ON HAS-BEENS.
SPORTS
I'VE SEEN YOUR BOYS. THEY TAKE THE HITS.
GUARANTEE TWO ROUNDS EACH. SHOVEL THEM IN, SHOVEL THEM OUT.
THEN SEW THEM TOGETHER FOR THE NEXT TIME.

THAT'S THE ONLY WAY TO DO IT. MONTH OR SO FROM NOW MAYBE I'LL SIGN YOU AT THE BACK DOOR.

HORSE RACE RESULTS

Chairman of the Board Noses Out Orchestral in 3rd

The Post

Bolie Jackson - Tonight

WHY NOT? YOU'RE LONG GONE, BOLIE.

YOU'VE HAD IT. WAIT'LL AFTER TONIGHT. YOU'LL WANT TO GET IN THE STABLE TOO.

ALL YOU HAVE TO DO IS GUARANTEE TWO ROUNDS.

TWO, THREE PRELIMS EVERY MONTH.

The Post

Resident Invites Musicians

Dog Fighting Ring Uncovered, Two Arrested

DO THAT STANDING ON YOUR HEAD, CAN'T YOU?

EASY, BOLIE...

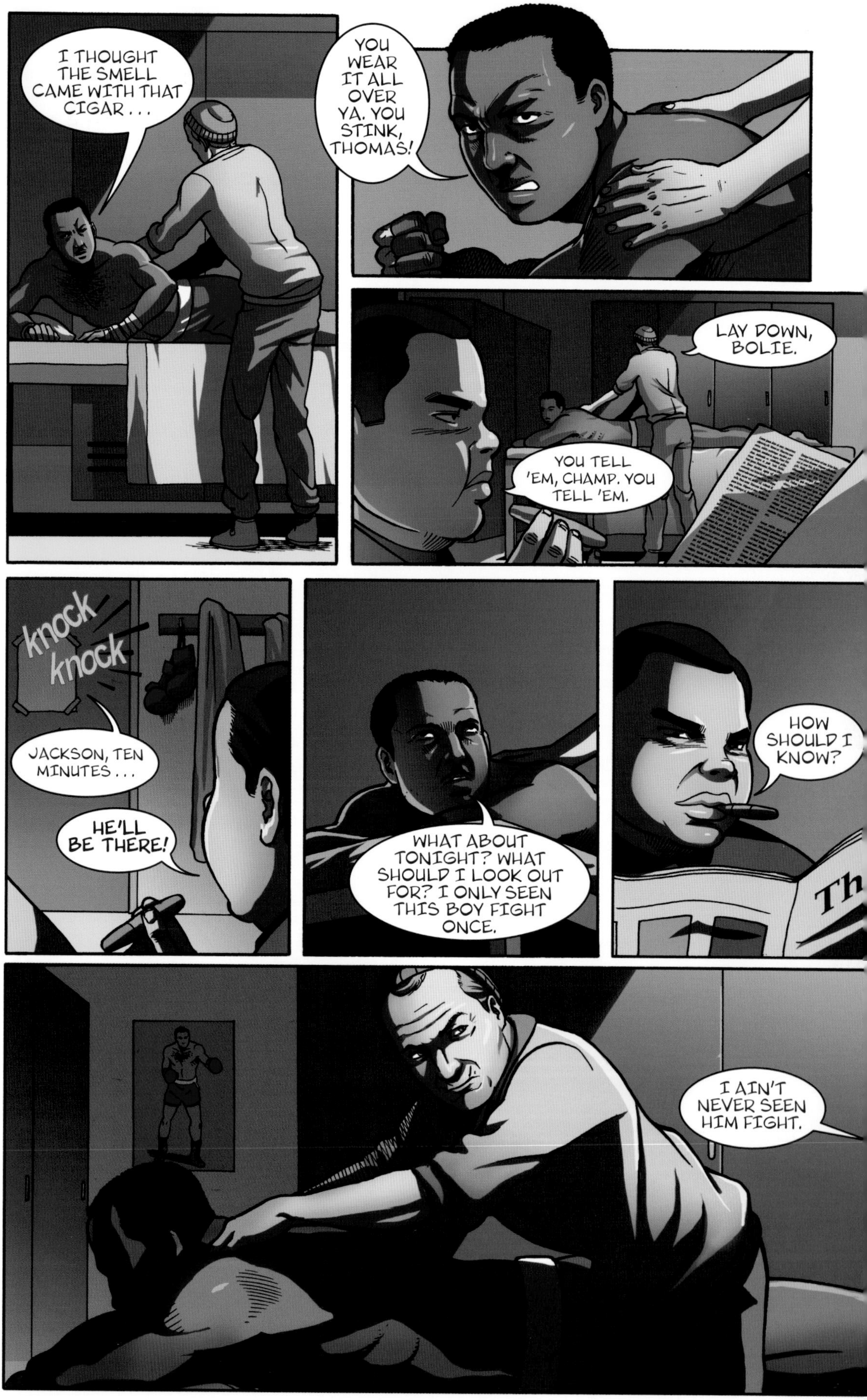
I THOUGHT THE SMELL CAME WITH THAT CIGAR . . .
YOU WEAR IT ALL OVER YA. YOU STINK, THOMAS!
LAY DOWN, BOLIE.
YOU TELL 'EM, CHAMP. YOU TELL 'EM.
knock knock
JACKSON, TEN MINUTES . . .
HE'LL BE THERE!
WHAT ABOUT TONIGHT? WHAT SHOULD I LOOK OUT FOR? I ONLY SEEN THIS BOY FIGHT ONCE.
HOW SHOULD I KNOW?
I AIN'T NEVER SEEN HIM FIGHT.

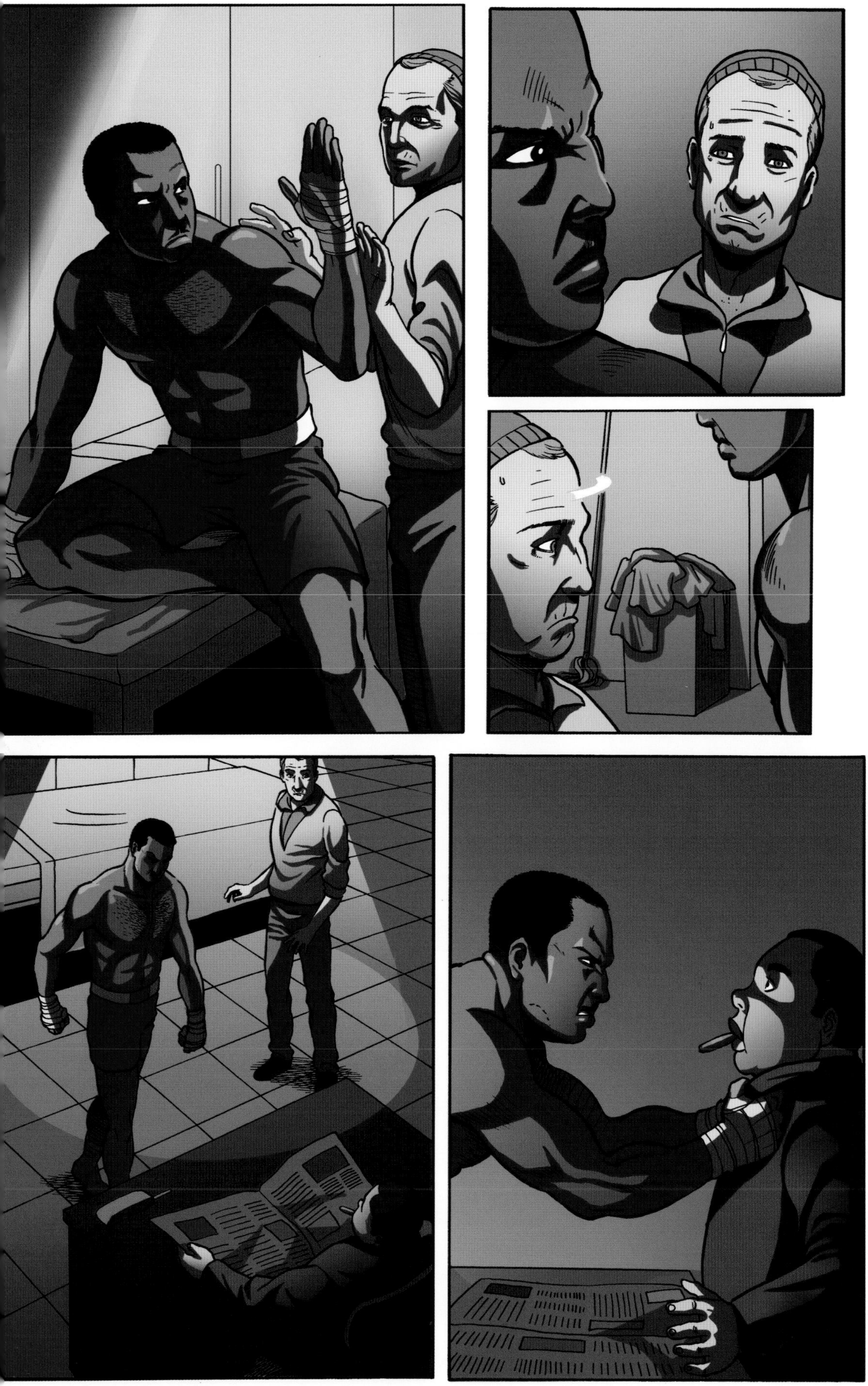

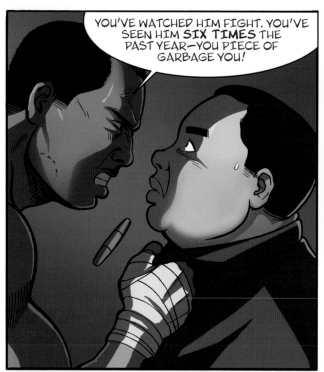

YOU'VE WATCHED HIM FIGHT. YOU'VE SEEN HIM **SIX TIMES** THE PAST YEAR—YOU PIECE OF GARBAGE YOU!

YOU GOT A BET ON **HIM**, DON'T YOU?

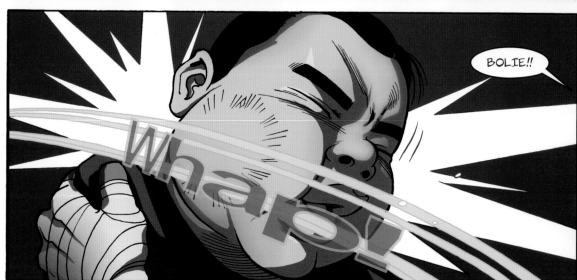

BOLIE!!

Whap!

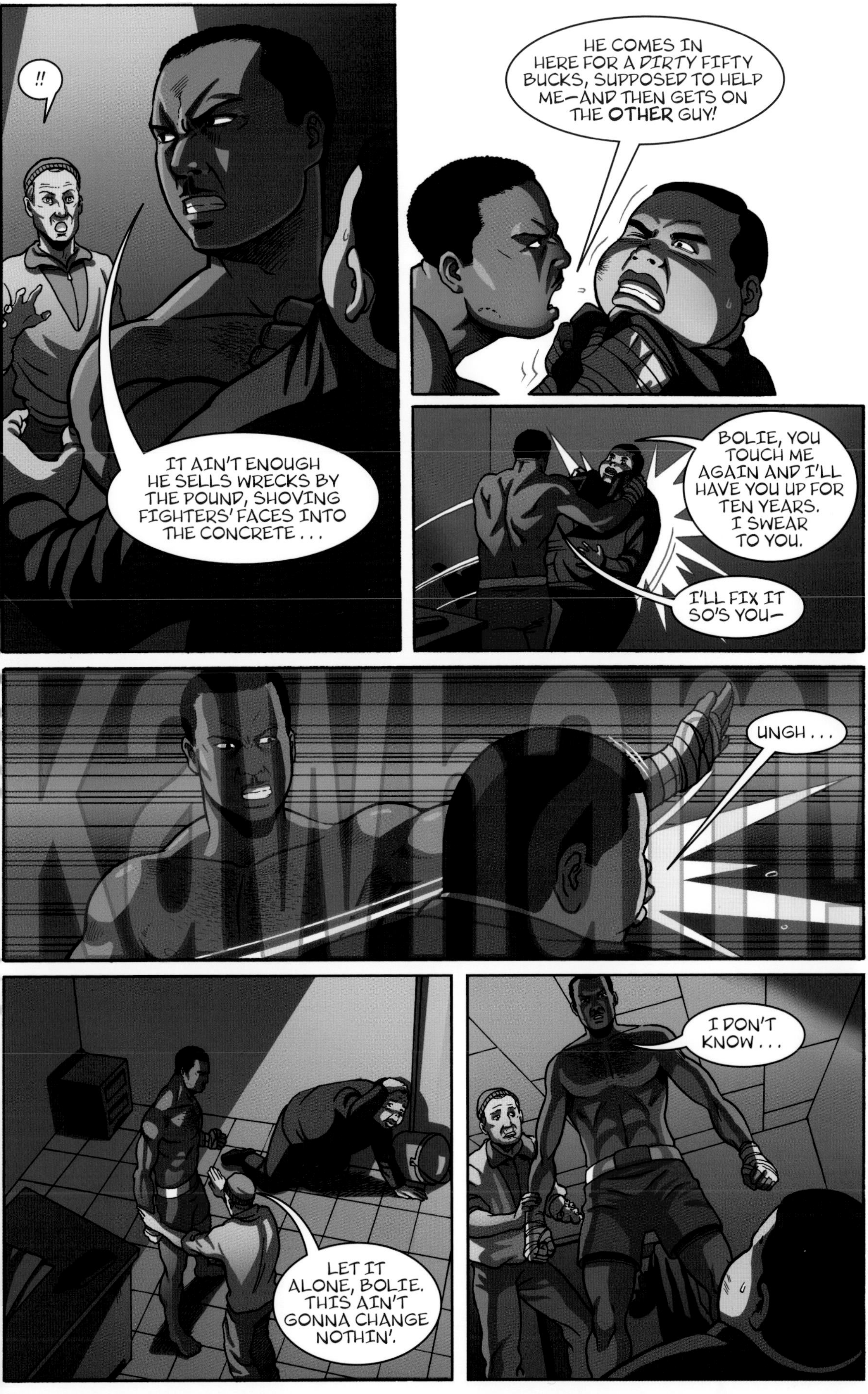
!!
IT AIN'T ENOUGH HE SELLS WRECKS BY THE POUND, SHOVING FIGHTERS' FACES INTO THE CONCRETE . . .
HE COMES IN HERE FOR A DIRTY FIFTY BUCKS, SUPPOSED TO HELP ME—AND THEN GETS ON THE OTHER GUY!
BOLIE, YOU TOUCH ME AGAIN AND I'LL HAVE YOU UP FOR TEN YEARS. I SWEAR TO YOU.
I'LL FIX IT SO'S YOU—
UNGH . . .
LET IT ALONE, BOLIE. THIS AIN'T GONNA CHANGE NOTHIN'.
I DON'T KNOW . . .

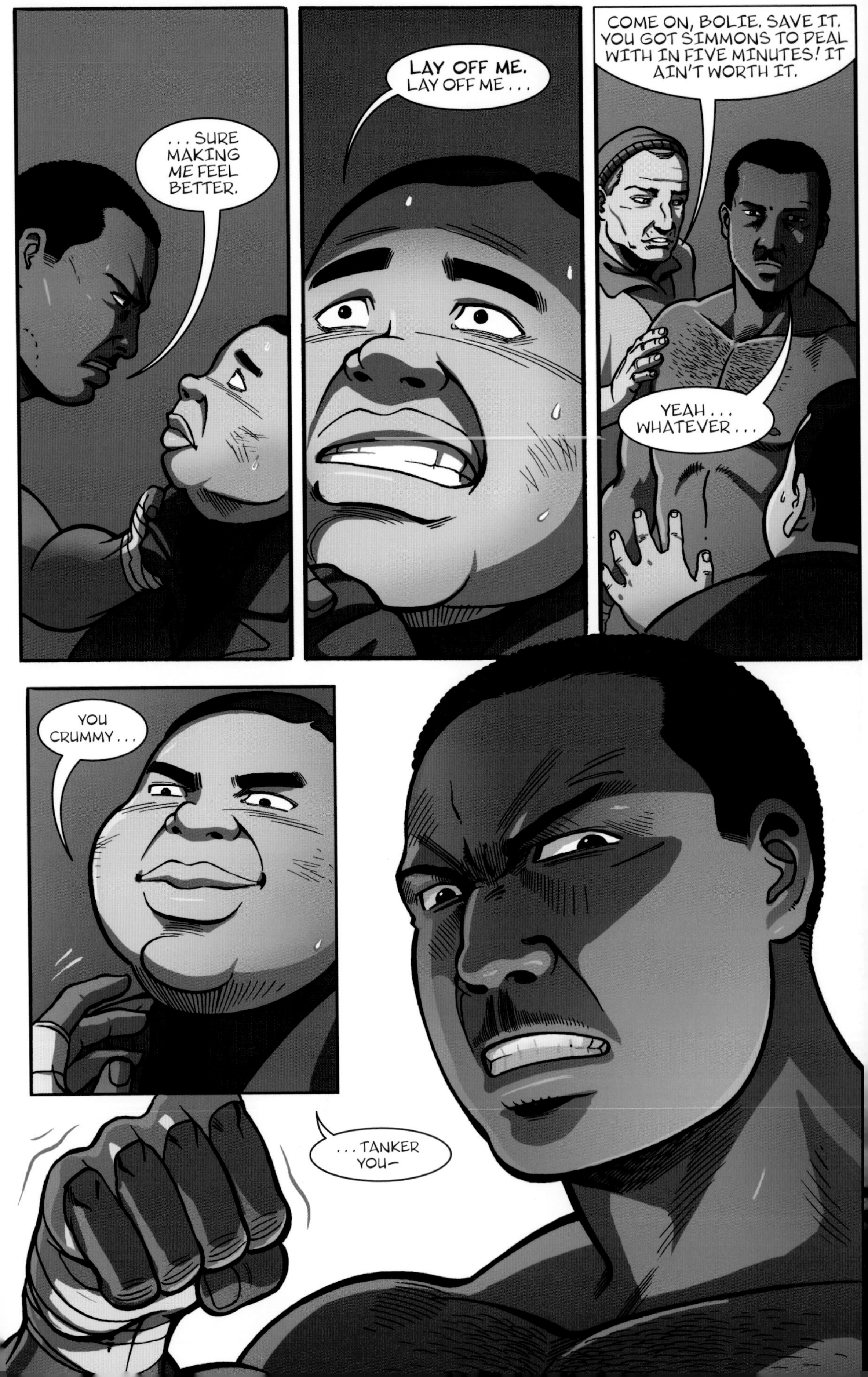
. . . SURE MAKING ME FEEL BETTER.
LAY OFF ME. LAY OFF ME . . .
COME ON, BOLIE. SAVE IT. YOU GOT SIMMONS TO DEAL WITH IN FIVE MINUTES! IT AIN'T WORTH IT.
YEAH . . . WHATEVER . . .
YOU CRUMMY . . .
. . . TANKER YOU—

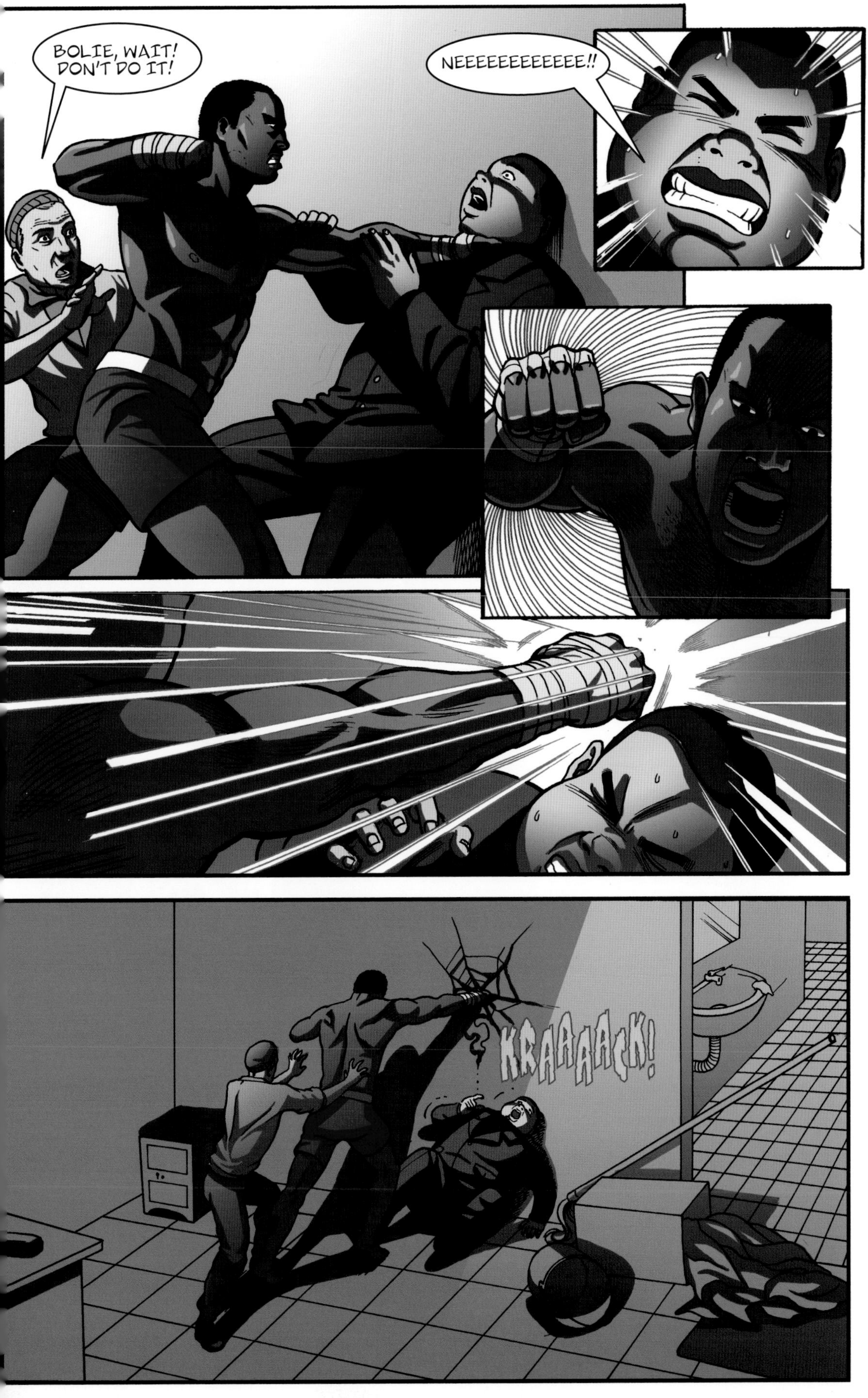
BOLIE, WAIT! DON'T DO IT!
NEEEEEEEEEEEE!!
KRAAAACK!

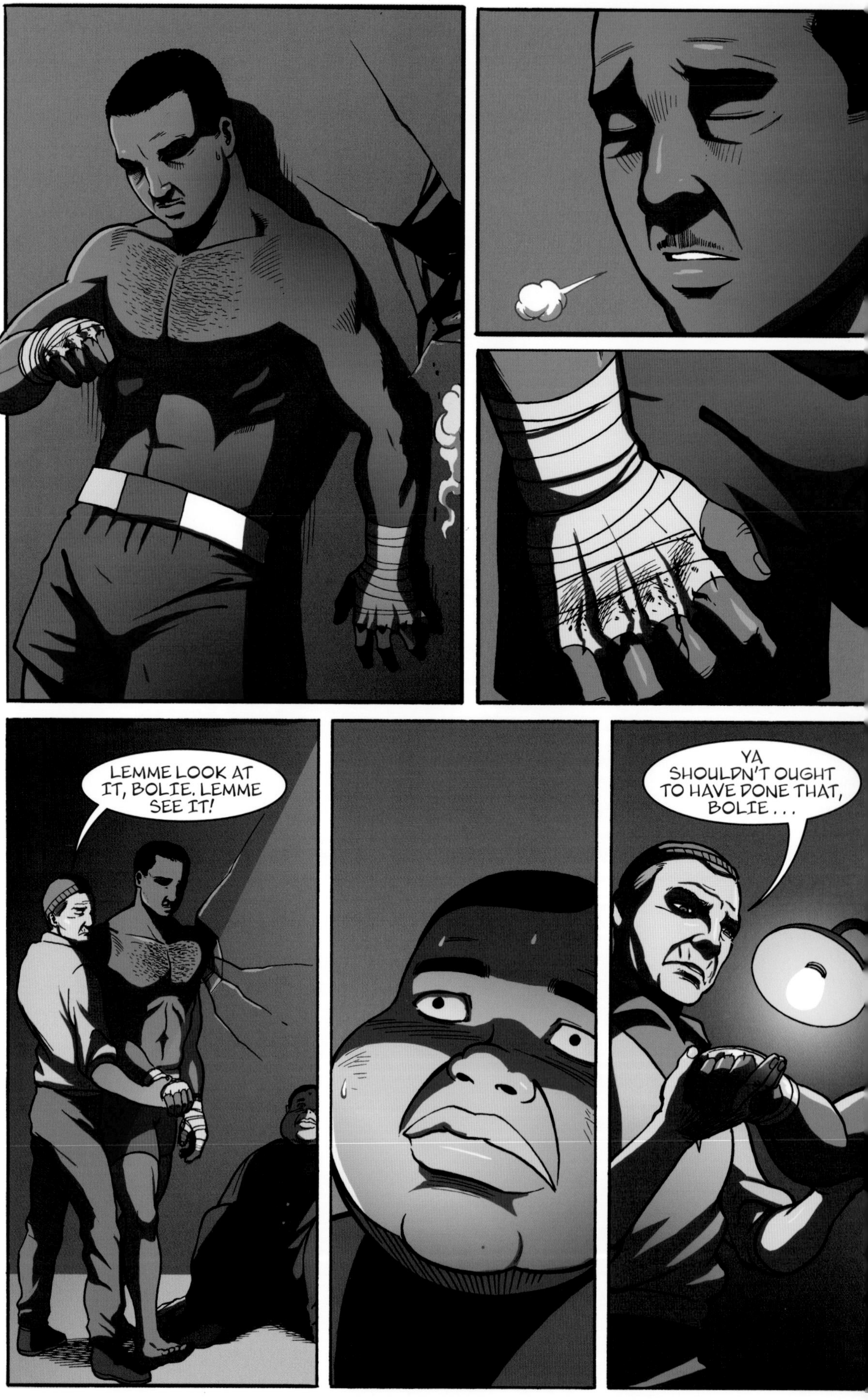
LEMME LOOK AT IT, BOLIE. LEMME SEE IT!
YA SHOULDN'T OUGHT TO HAVE DONE THAT, BOLIE . . .

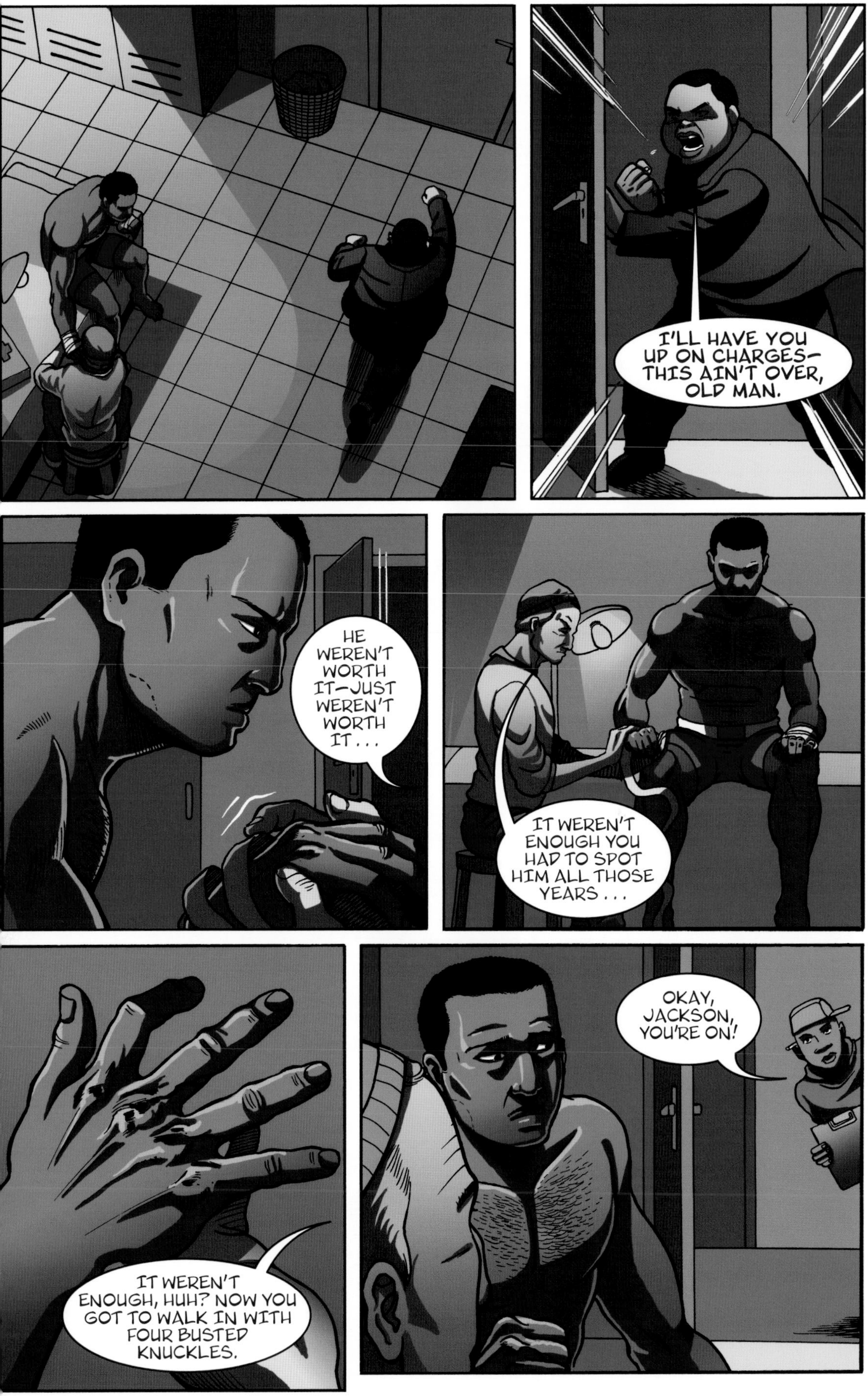
I'LL HAVE YOU UP ON CHARGES— THIS AIN'T OVER, OLD MAN.
HE WEREN'T WORTH IT—JUST WEREN'T WORTH IT . . .
IT WEREN'T ENOUGH YOU HAD TO SPOT HIM ALL THOSE YEARS . . .
IT WEREN'T ENOUGH, HUH? NOW YOU GOT TO WALK IN WITH FOUR BUSTED KNUCKLES.
OKAY, JACKSON, YOU'RE ON!

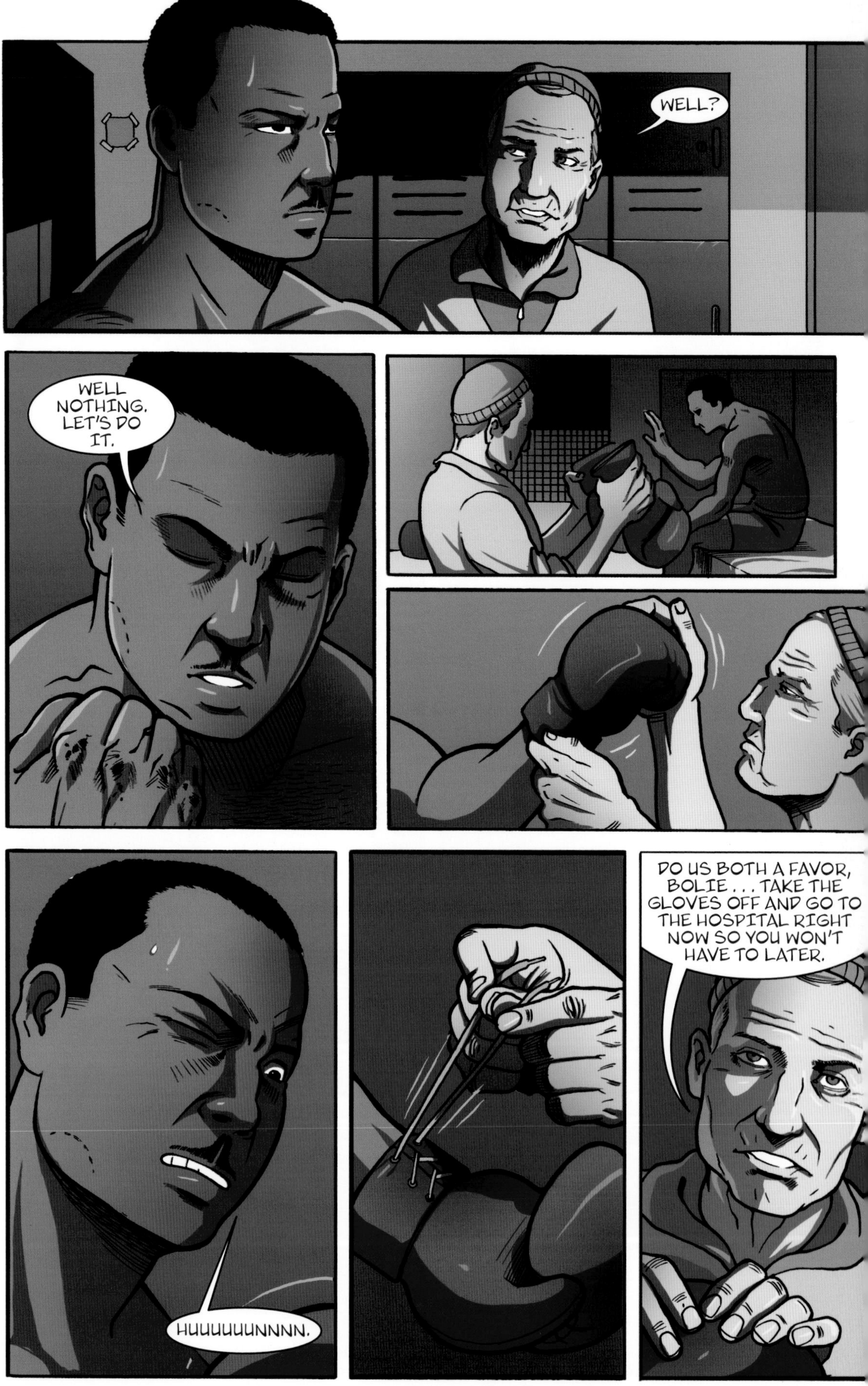
WELL?
WELL NOTHING. LET'S DO IT.
HUUUUUUNNNN.
DO US BOTH A FAVOR, BOLIE . . . TAKE THE GLOVES OFF AND GO TO THE HOSPITAL RIGHT NOW SO YOU WON'T HAVE TO LATER.

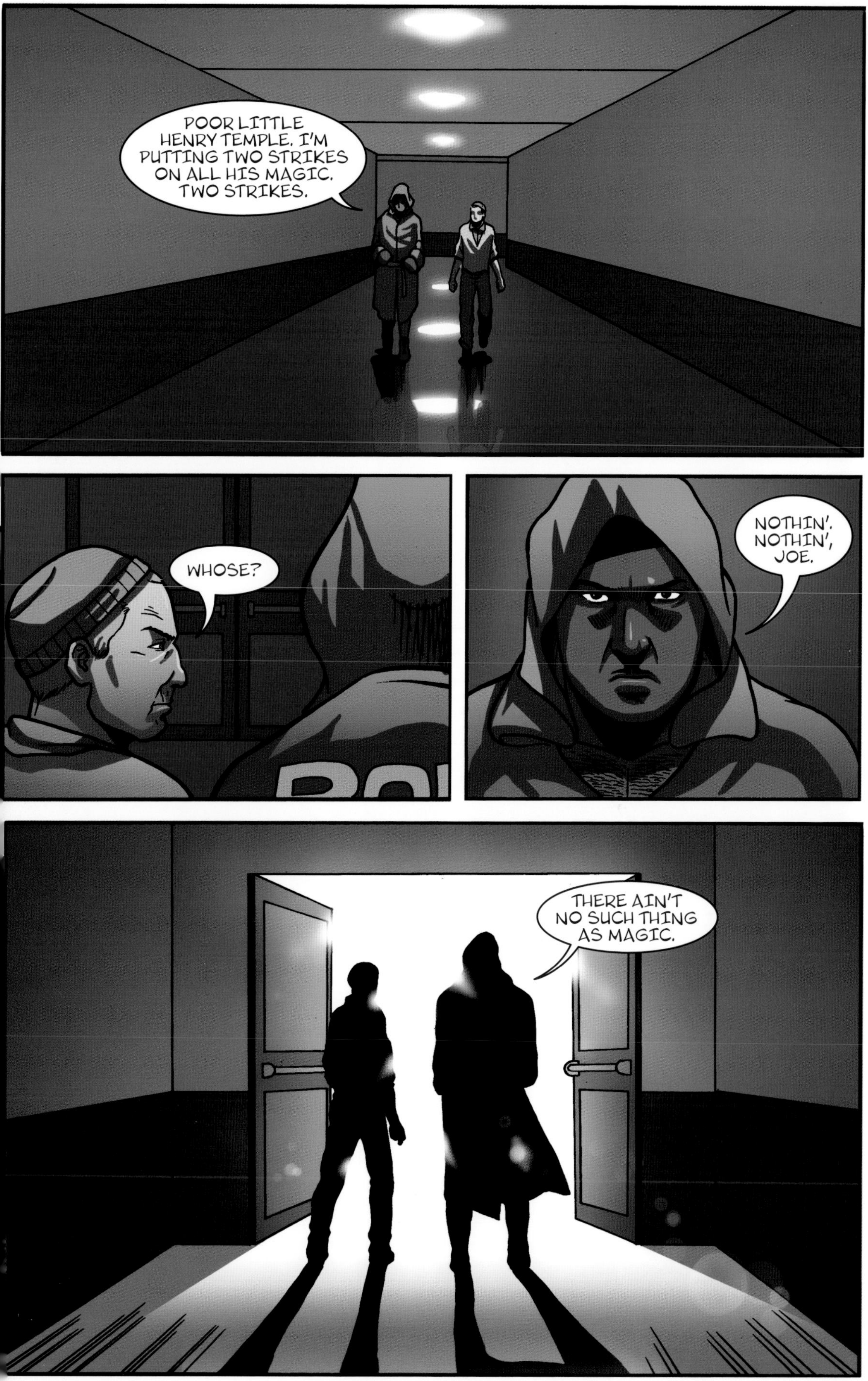
POOR LITTLE HENRY TEMPLE. I'M PUTTING TWO STRIKES ON ALL HIS MAGIC. TWO STRIKES.
WHOSE?
NOTHIN'. NOTHIN', JOE.
THERE AIN'T NO SUCH THING AS MAGIC.

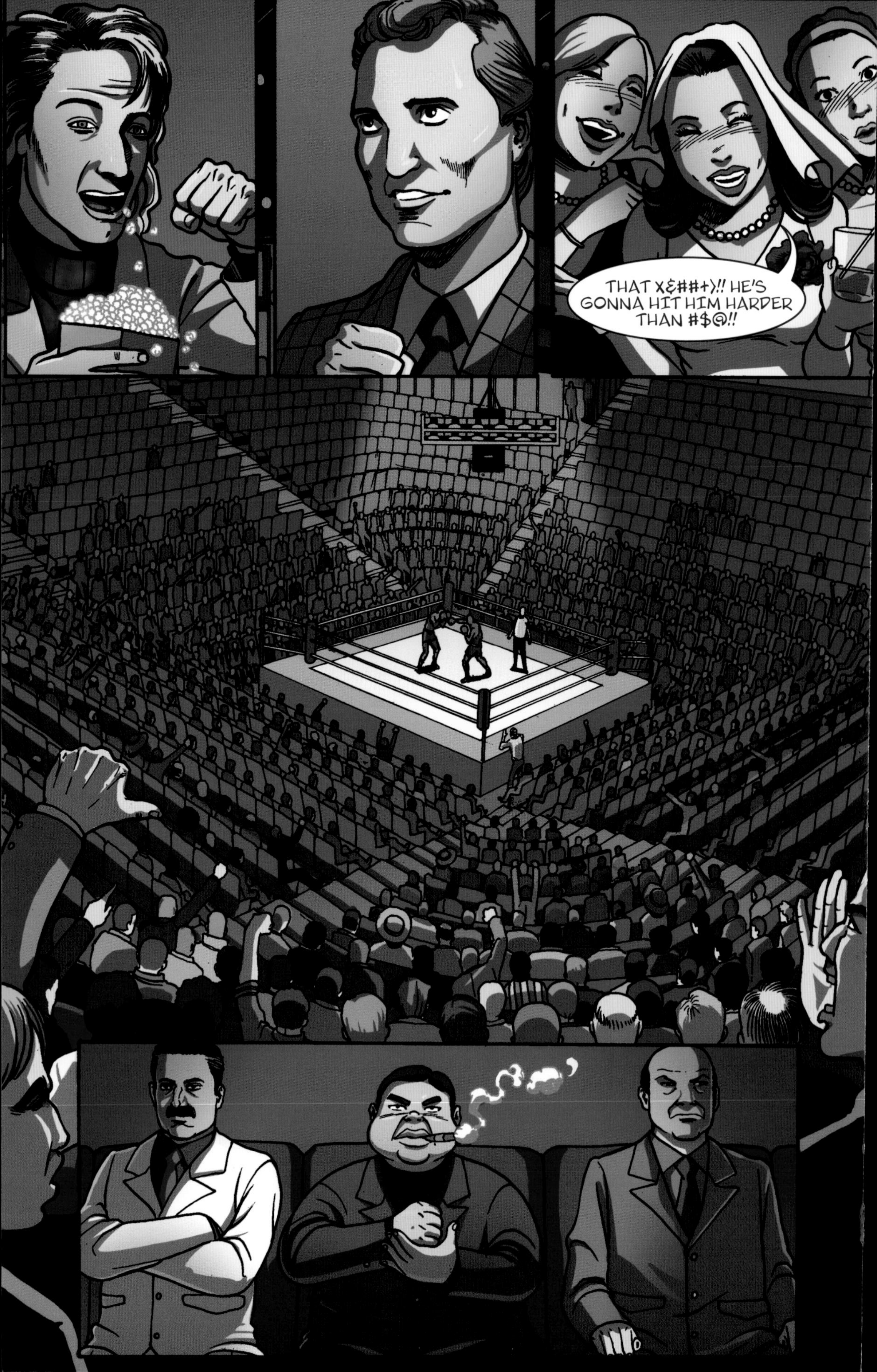
THAT X&##+)!! HE'S GONNA HIT HIM HARDER THAN #$@!!

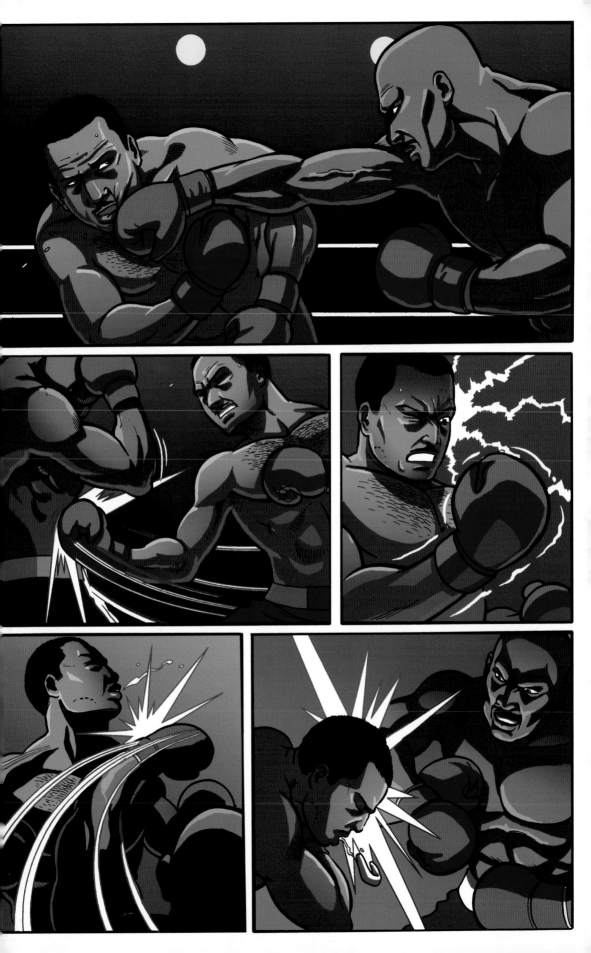

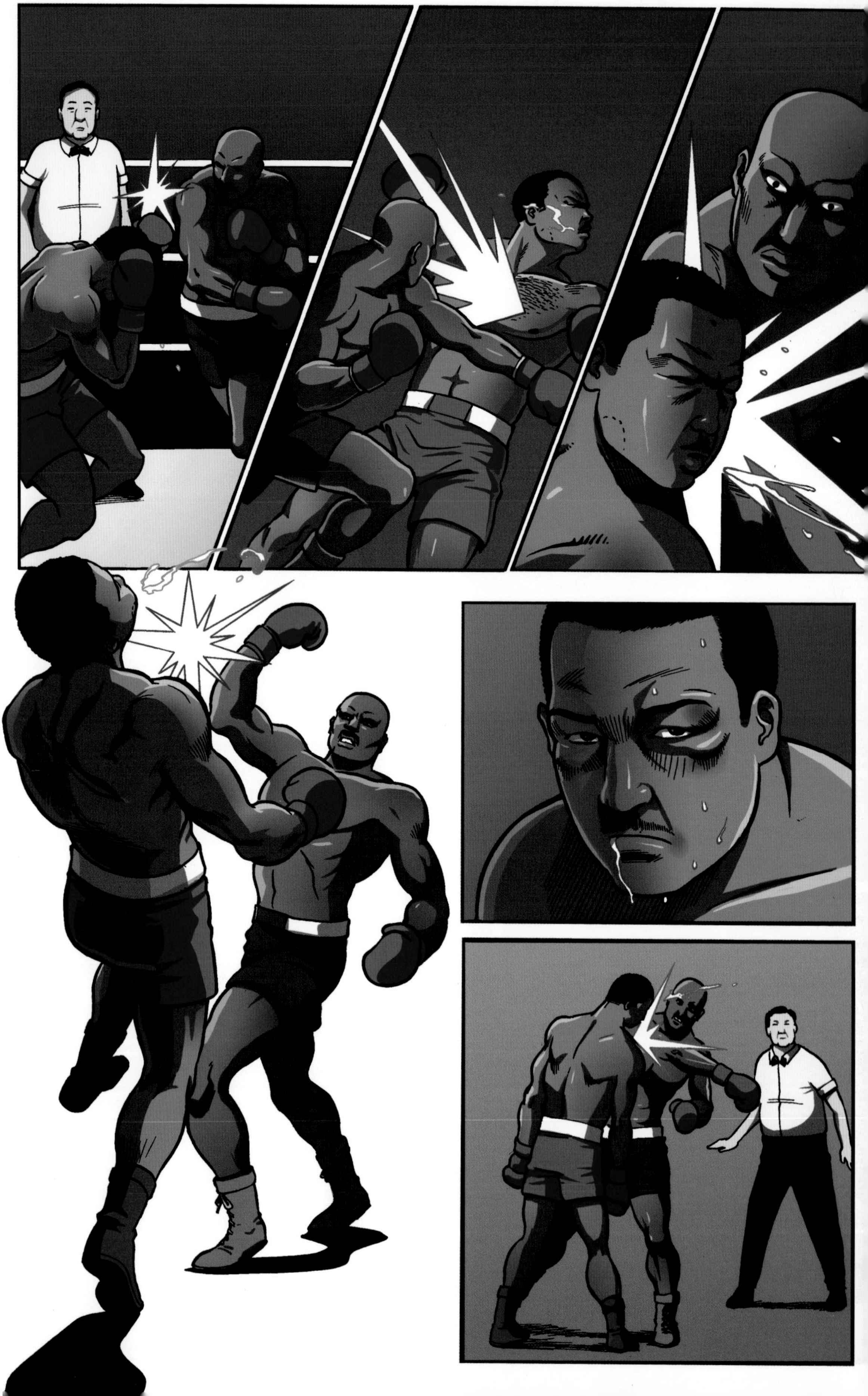

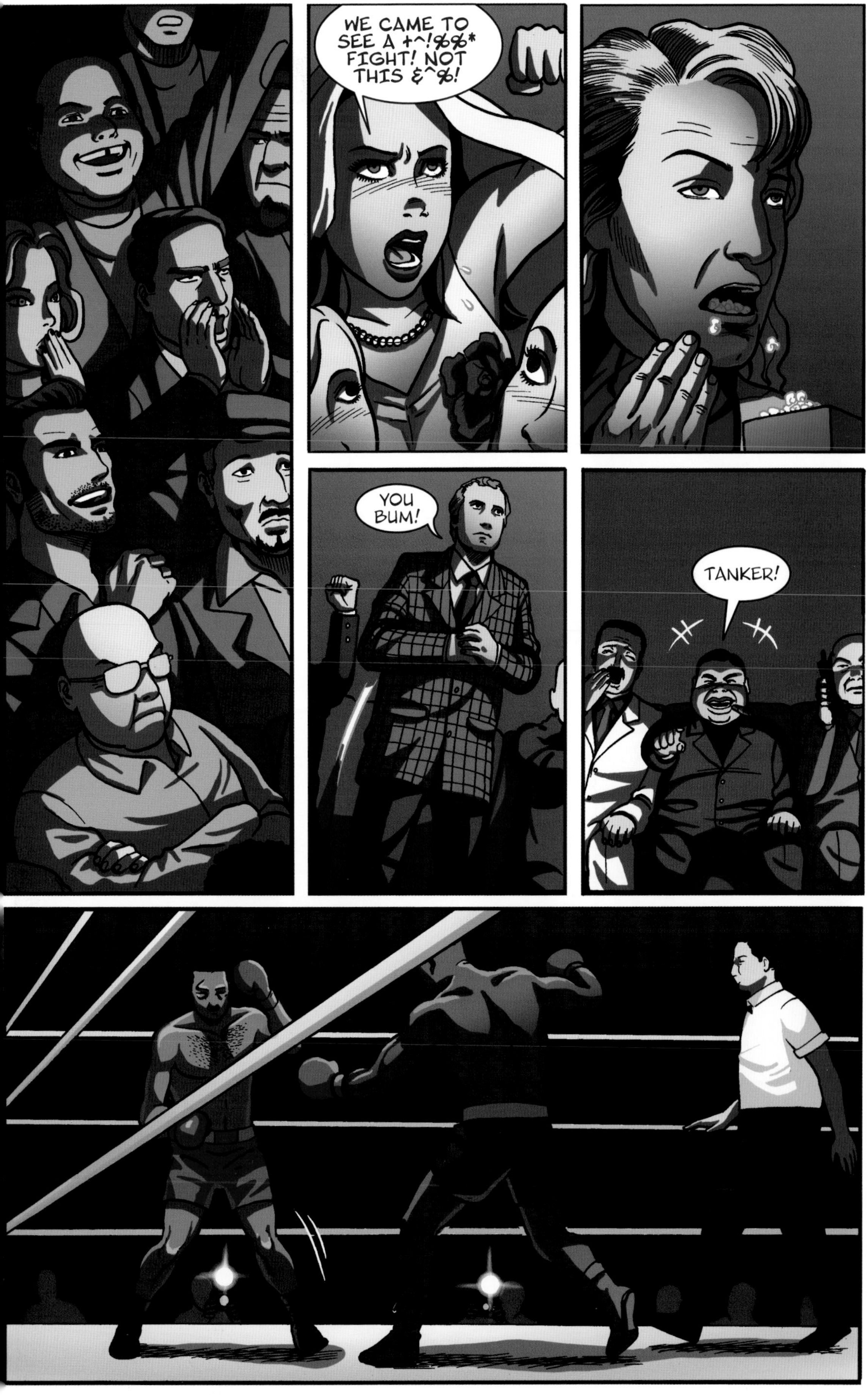

WE CAME TO SEE A +^!%%* FIGHT! NOT THIS &^%!
YOU BUM!
TANKER!

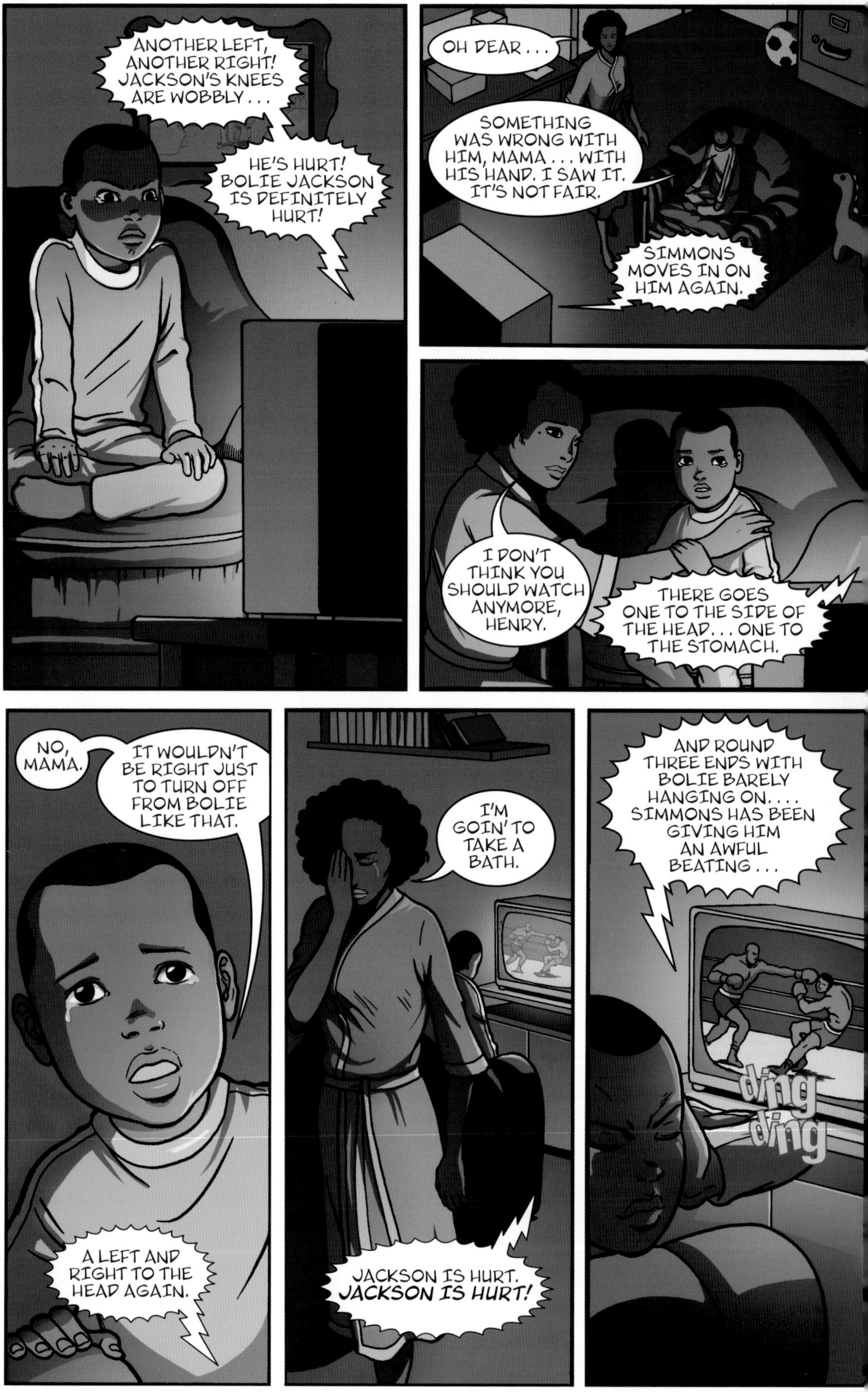

ANOTHER LEFT, ANOTHER RIGHT! JACKSON'S KNEES ARE WOBBLY . . .
HE'S HURT! BOLIE JACKSON IS DEFINITELY HURT!
OH DEAR . . .
SOMETHING WAS WRONG WITH HIM, MAMA . . . WITH HIS HAND. I SAW IT. IT'S NOT FAIR.
SIMMONS MOVES IN ON HIM AGAIN.
I DON'T THINK YOU SHOULD WATCH ANYMORE, HENRY.
THERE GOES ONE TO THE SIDE OF THE HEAD. . . ONE TO THE STOMACH.
NO, MAMA.
IT WOULDN'T BE RIGHT JUST TO TURN OFF FROM BOLIE LIKE THAT.
A LEFT AND RIGHT TO THE HEAD AGAIN.
I'M GOIN' TO TAKE A BATH.
JACKSON IS HURT. JACKSON IS HURT!
AND ROUND THREE ENDS WITH BOLIE BARELY HANGING ON. . . . SIMMONS HAS BEEN GIVING HIM AN AWFUL BEATING . . .
ding ding

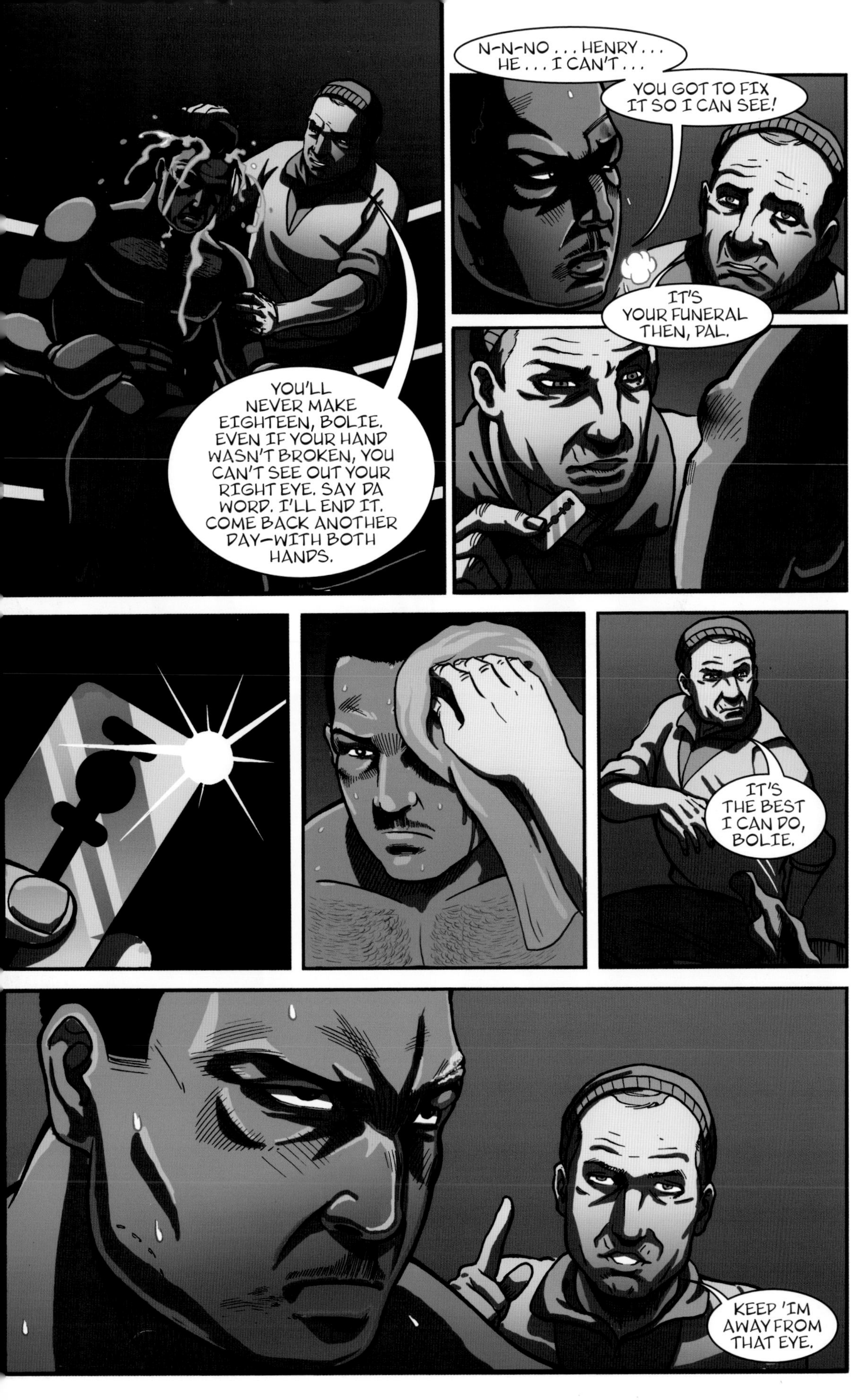

YOU'LL NEVER MAKE EIGHTEEN, BOLIE. EVEN IF YOUR HAND WASN'T BROKEN, YOU CAN'T SEE OUT YOUR RIGHT EYE. SAY DA WORD. I'LL END IT. COME BACK ANOTHER DAY—WITH BOTH HANDS.
N-N-NO . . . HENRY . . . HE . . . I CAN'T . . .
YOU GOT TO FIX IT SO I CAN SEE!
IT'S YOUR FUNERAL THEN, PAL.
IT'S THE BEST I CAN DO, BOLIE.
KEEP 'IM AWAY FROM THAT EYE.

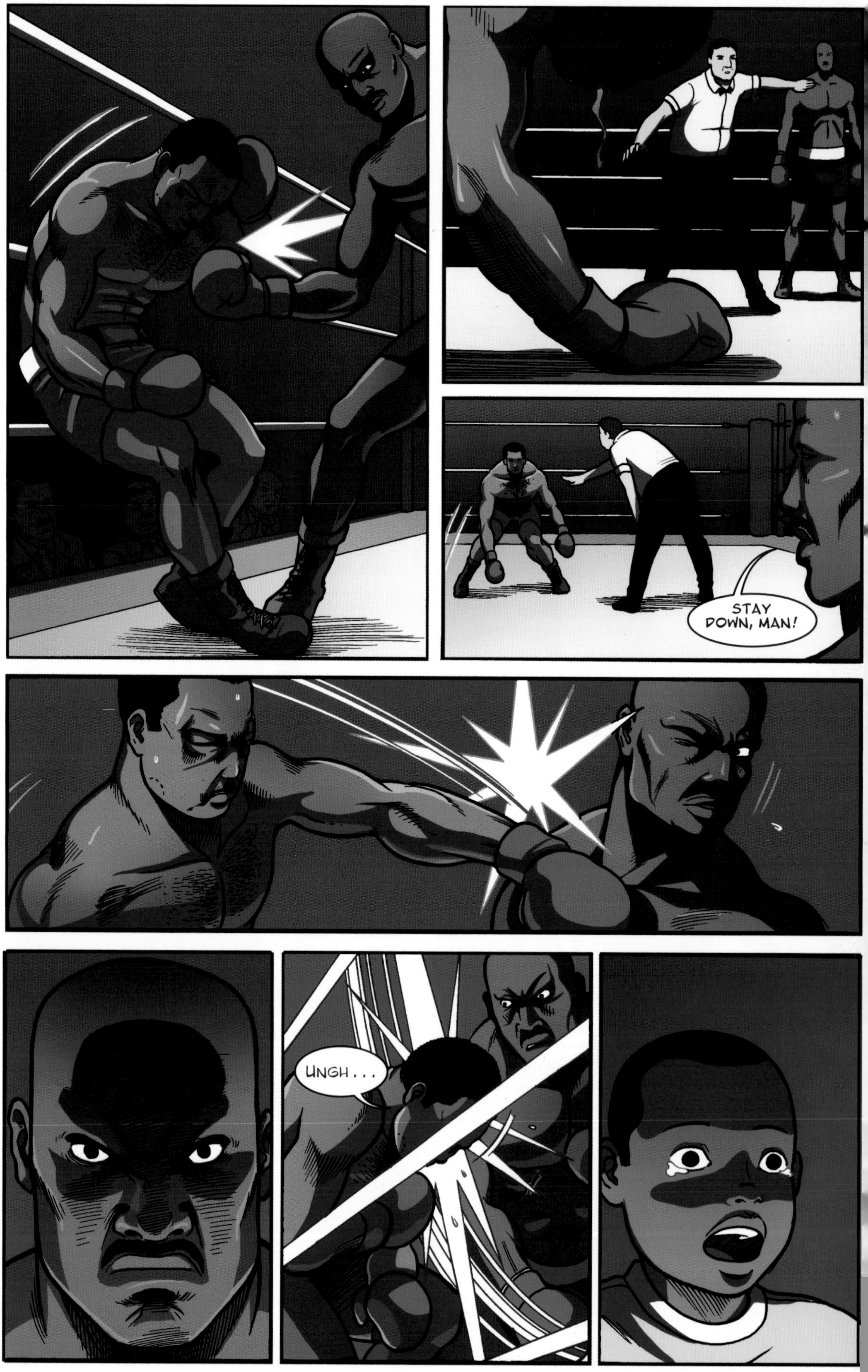
STAY DOWN, MAN!
UNGH . . .

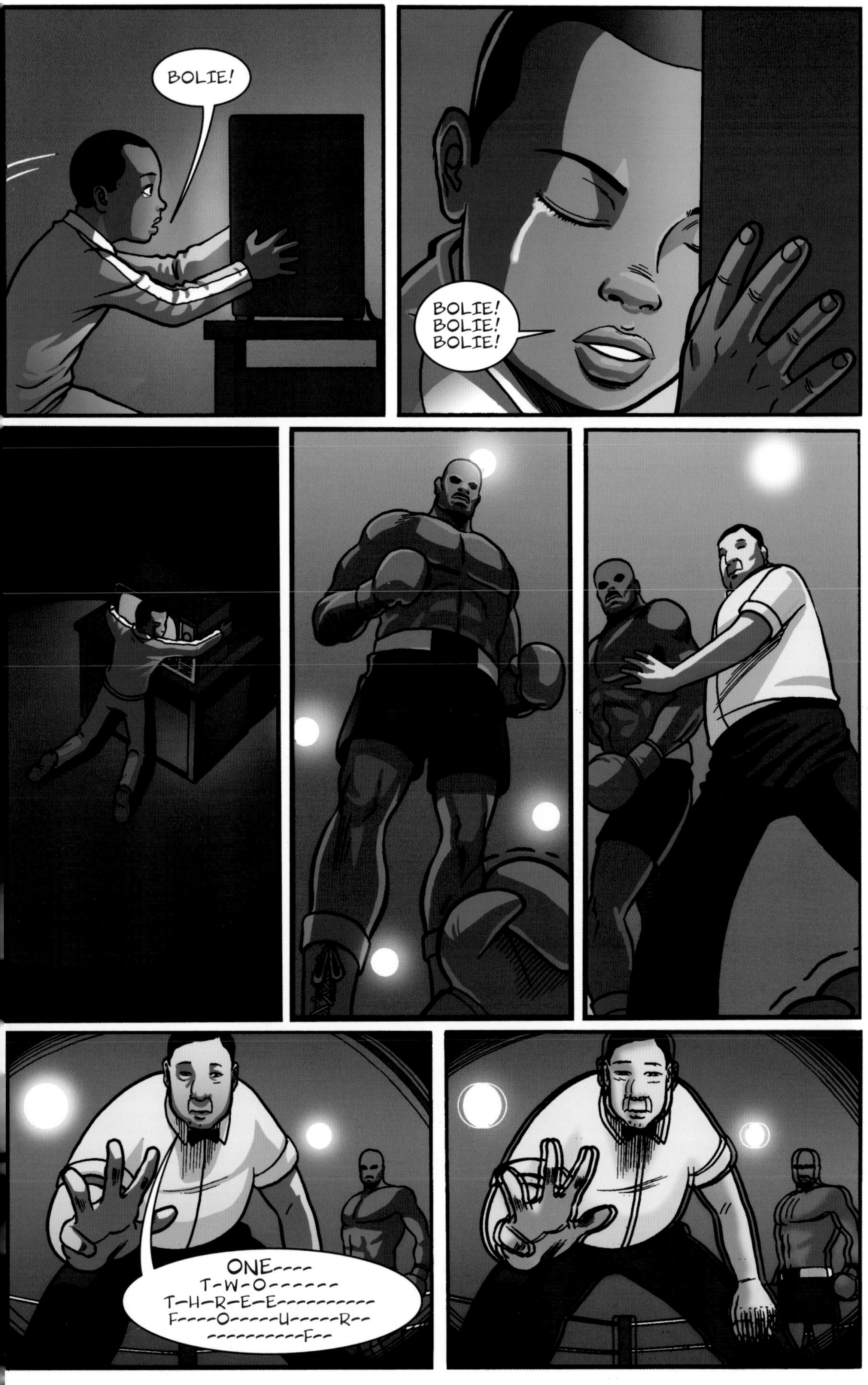
BOLIE!
BOLIE! BOLIE! BOLIE!
ONE---- T-W-O------- T-H-R-E-E----------- F----O-----U-----R-- -----------F--

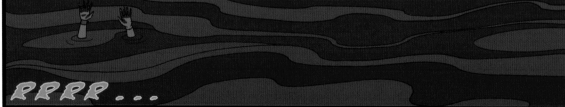

RRRR . . .

RRRIiiiiiiiiiii . . .

iiiiiiiiinnn

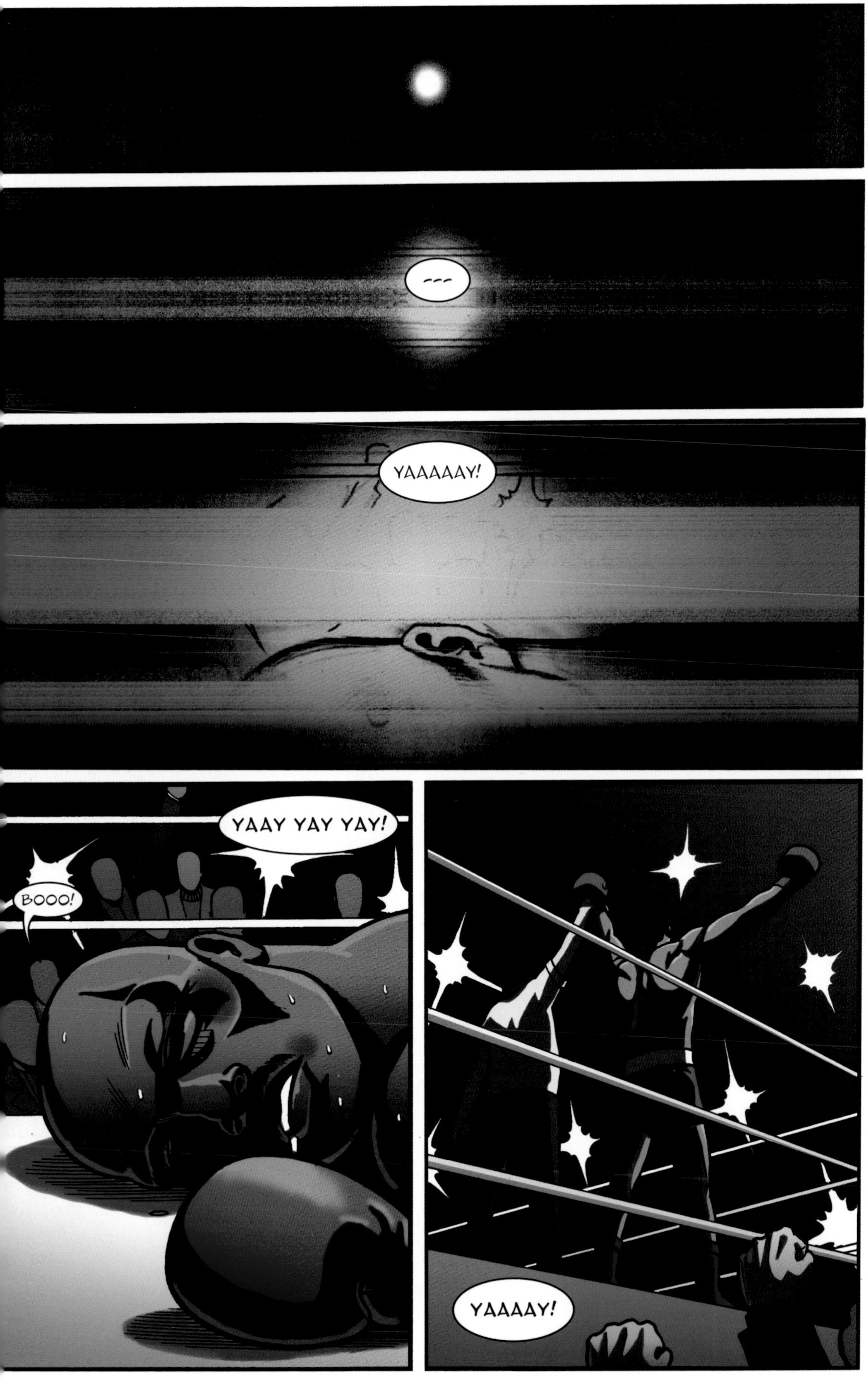

YAAAAAY!
YAAY YAY YAY!
BOOO!
YAAAAY!

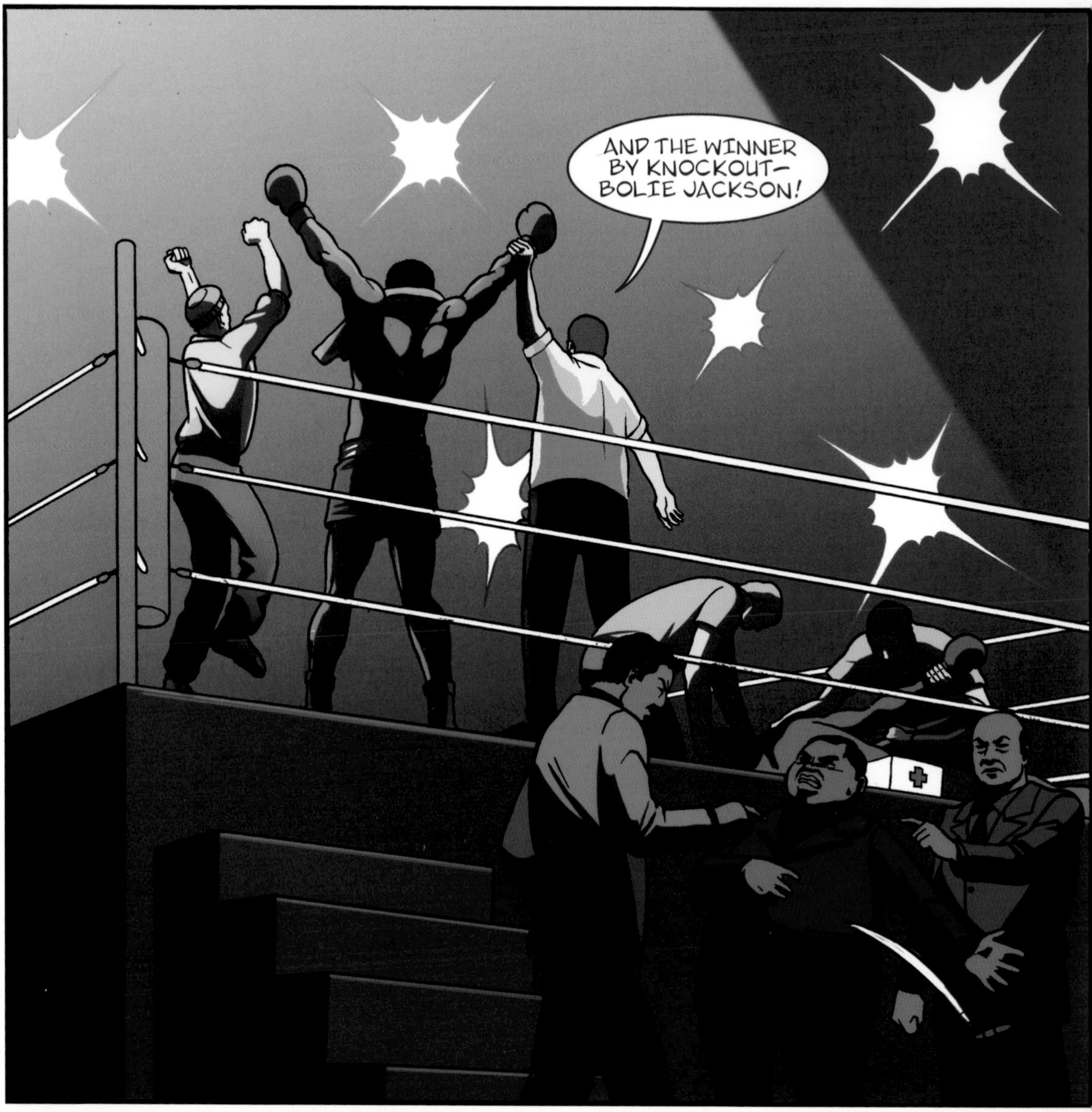
AND THE WINNER BY KNOCKOUT— BOLIE JACKSON!

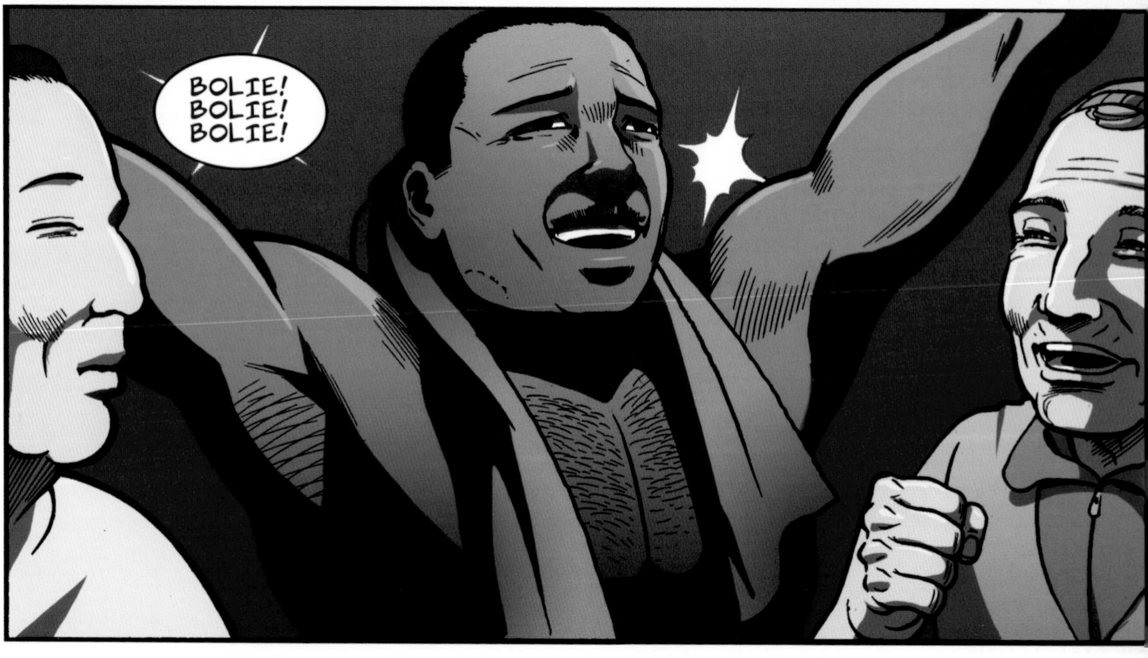
BOLIE! BOLIE! BOLIE!

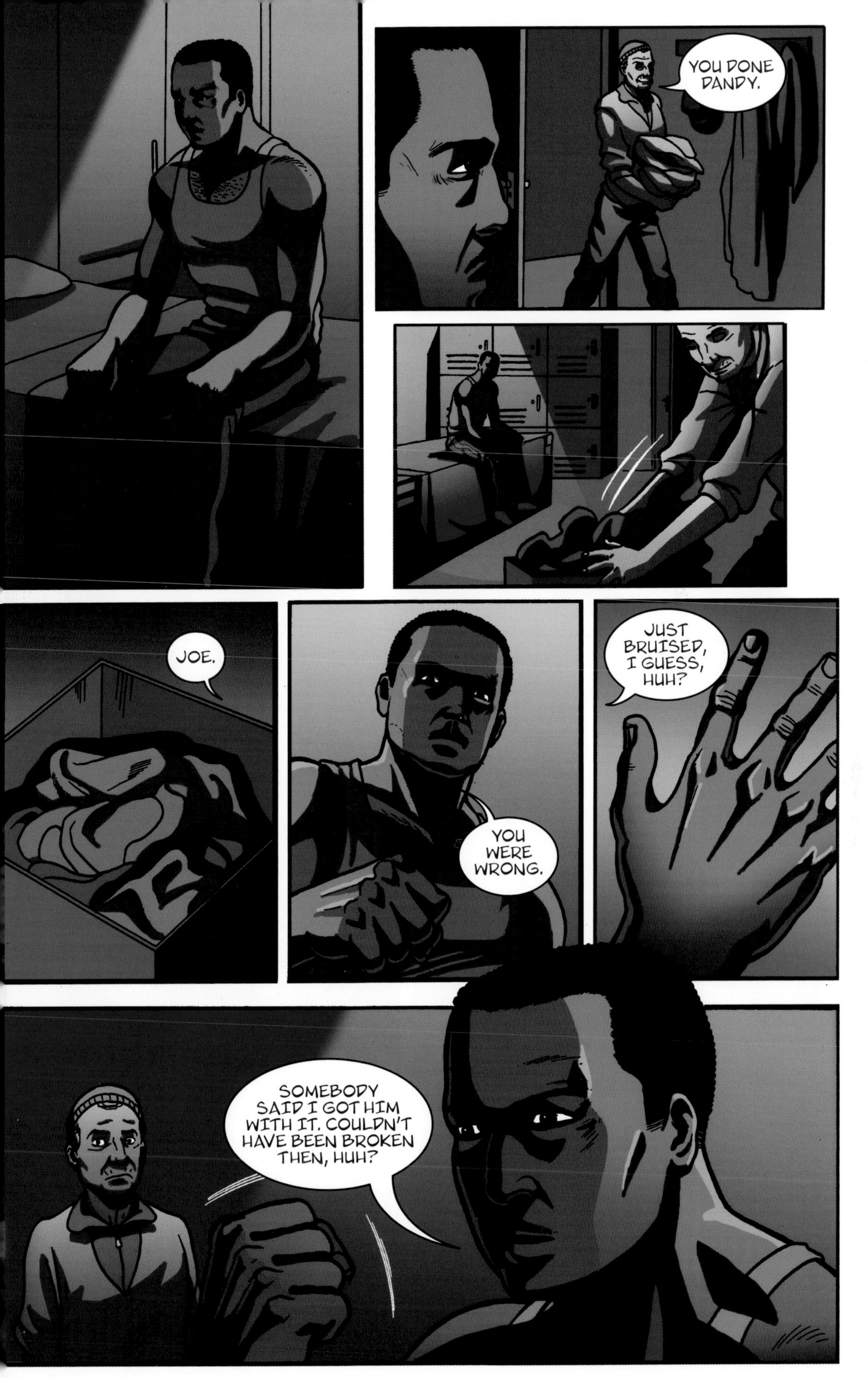
YOU DONE DANDY.
JOE.
YOU WERE WRONG.
JUST BRUISED, I GUESS, HUH?
SOMEBODY SAID I GOT HIM WITH IT. COULDN'T HAVE BEEN BROKEN THEN, HUH?

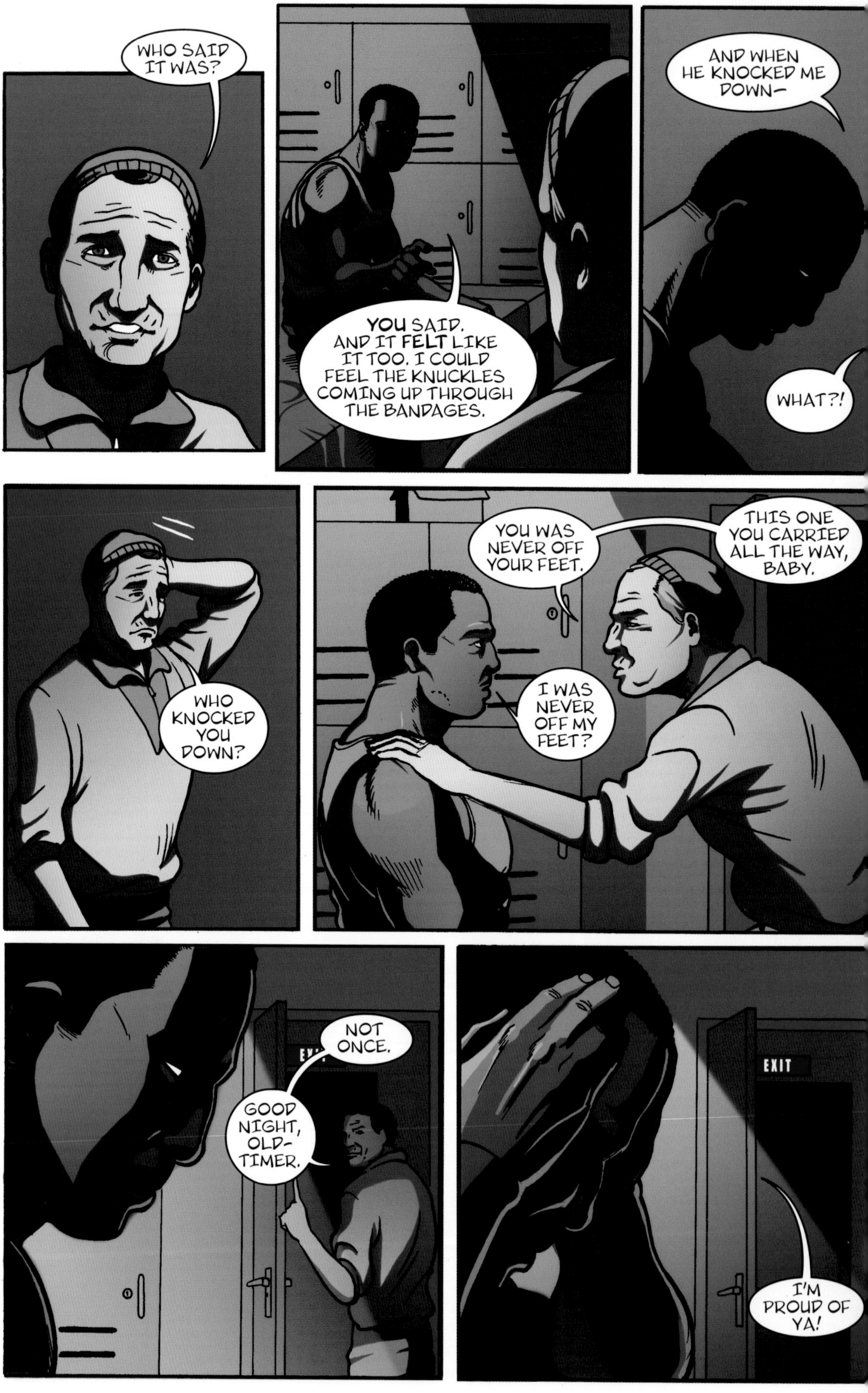
WHO SAID IT WAS?
YOU SAID. AND IT FELT LIKE IT TOO. I COULD FEEL THE KNUCKLES COMING UP THROUGH THE BANDAGES.
AND WHEN HE KNOCKED ME DOWN—
WHAT?!
WHO KNOCKED YOU DOWN?
YOU WAS NEVER OFF YOUR FEET.
THIS ONE YOU CARRIED ALL THE WAY, BABY.
I WAS NEVER OFF MY FEET?
NOT ONCE.
GOOD NIGHT, OLD-TIMER.
EXIT
I'M PROUD OF YA!

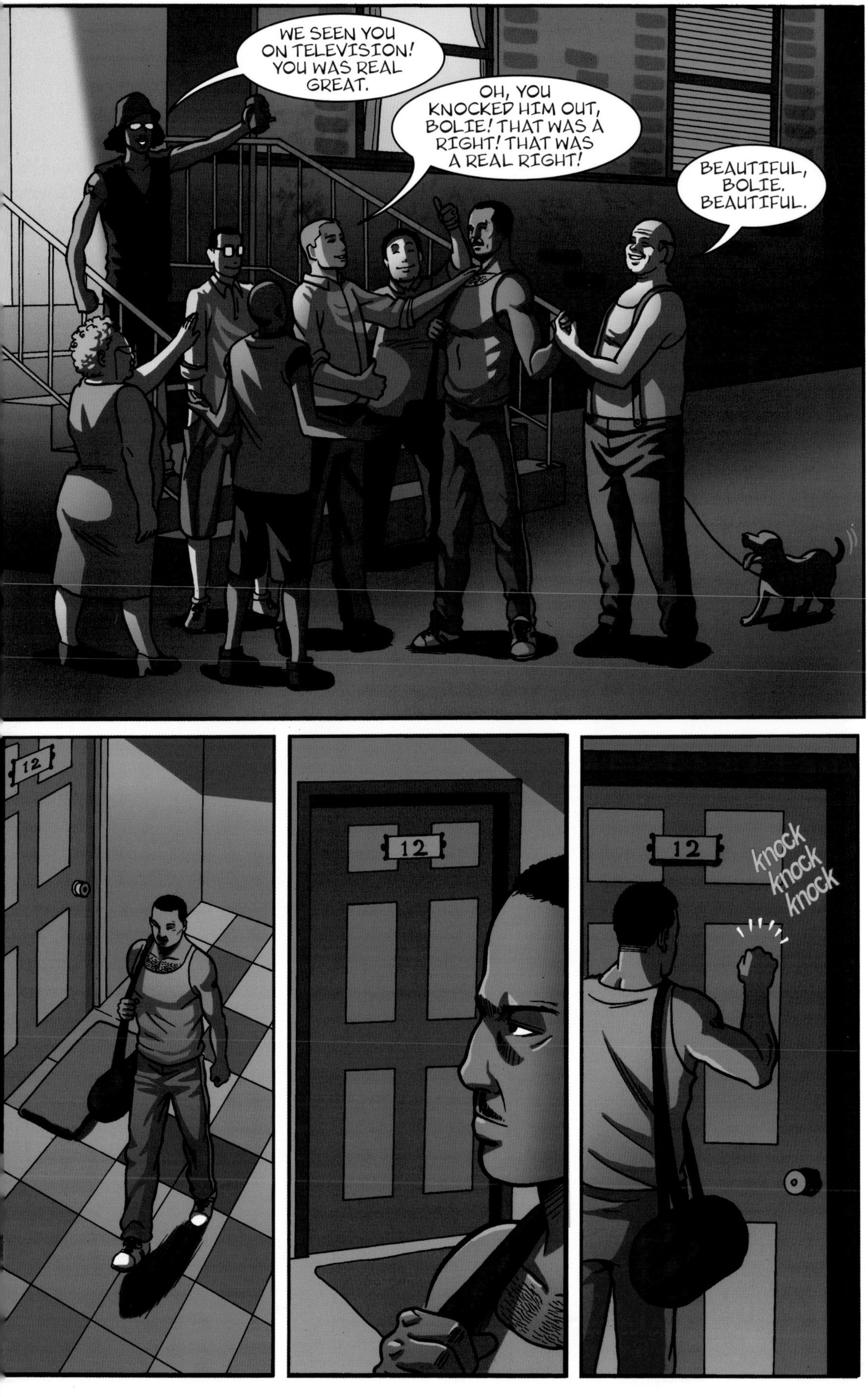
WE SEEN YOU ON TELEVISION! YOU WAS REAL GREAT.
OH, YOU KNOCKED HIM OUT, BOLIE! THAT WAS A RIGHT! THAT WAS A REAL RIGHT!
BEAUTIFUL, BOLIE. BEAUTIFUL.
12
12
12
knock knock knock

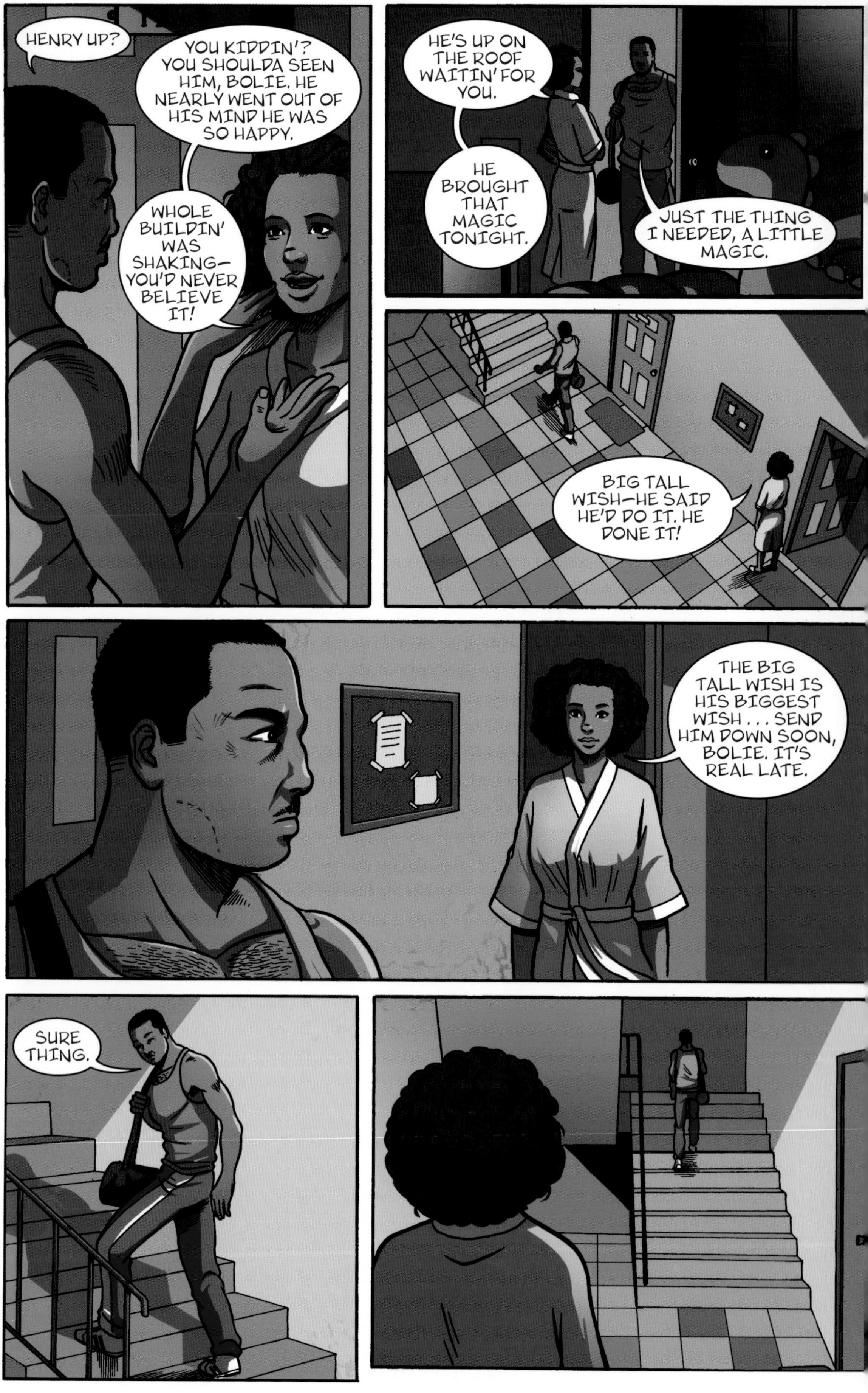
HENRY UP?
YOU KIDDIN'? YOU SHOULDA SEEN HIM, BOLIE. HE NEARLY WENT OUT OF HIS MIND HE WAS SO HAPPY.
WHOLE BUILDIN' WAS SHAKING—YOU'D NEVER BELIEVE IT!
HE'S UP ON THE ROOF WAITIN' FOR YOU.
HE BROUGHT THAT MAGIC TONIGHT.
JUST THE THING I NEEDED, A LITTLE MAGIC.
BIG TALL WISH—HE SAID HE'D DO IT. HE DONE IT!
THE BIG TALL WISH IS HIS BIGGEST WISH . . . SEND HIM DOWN SOON, BOLIE. IT'S REAL LATE.
SURE THING.

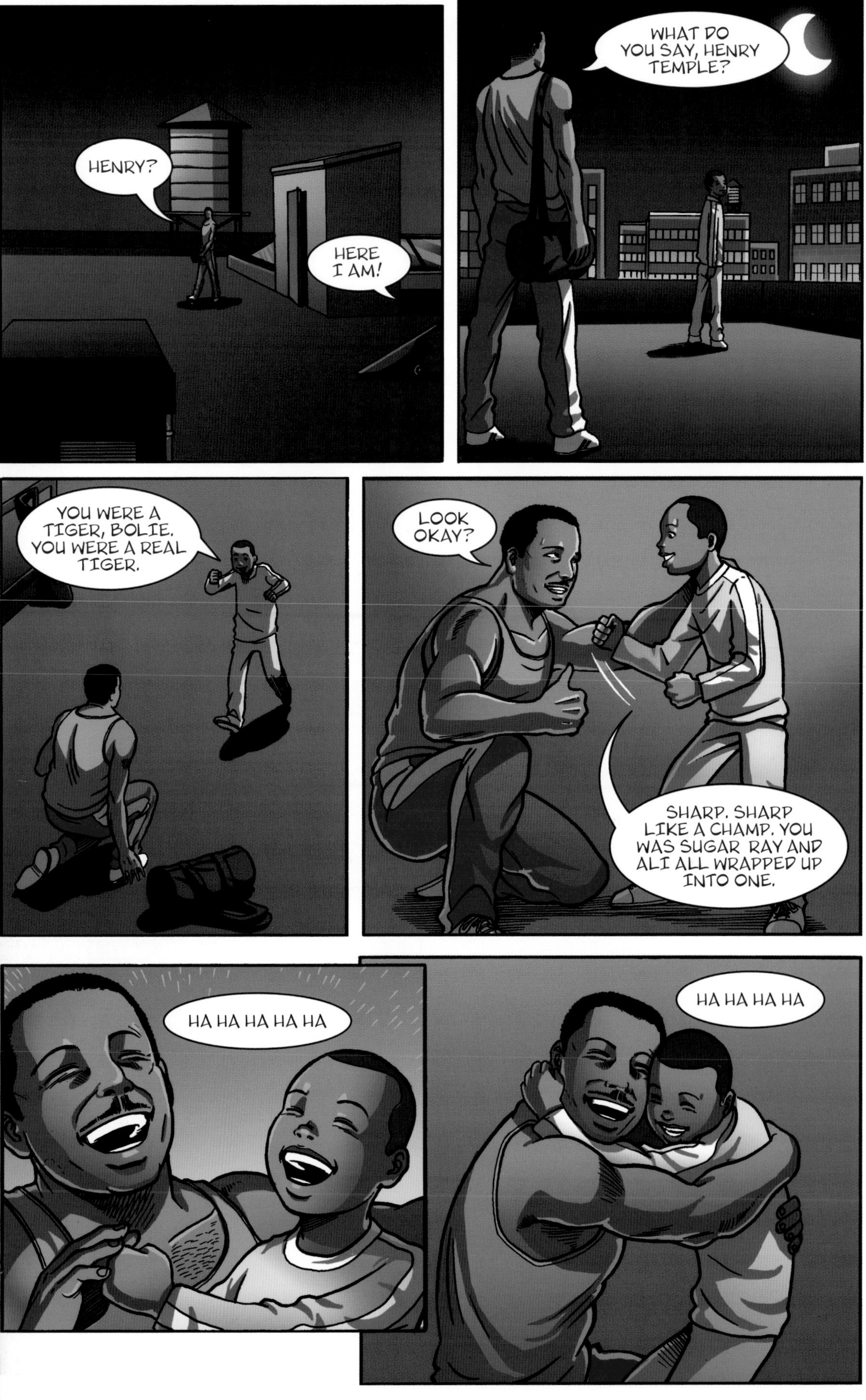
HENRY?
HERE I AM!
WHAT DO YOU SAY, HENRY TEMPLE?
YOU WERE A TIGER, BOLIE. YOU WERE A REAL TIGER.
LOOK OKAY?
SHARP. SHARP LIKE A CHAMP. YOU WAS SUGAR RAY AND ALI ALL WRAPPED UP INTO ONE.
HA HA HA HA HA
HA HA HA HA

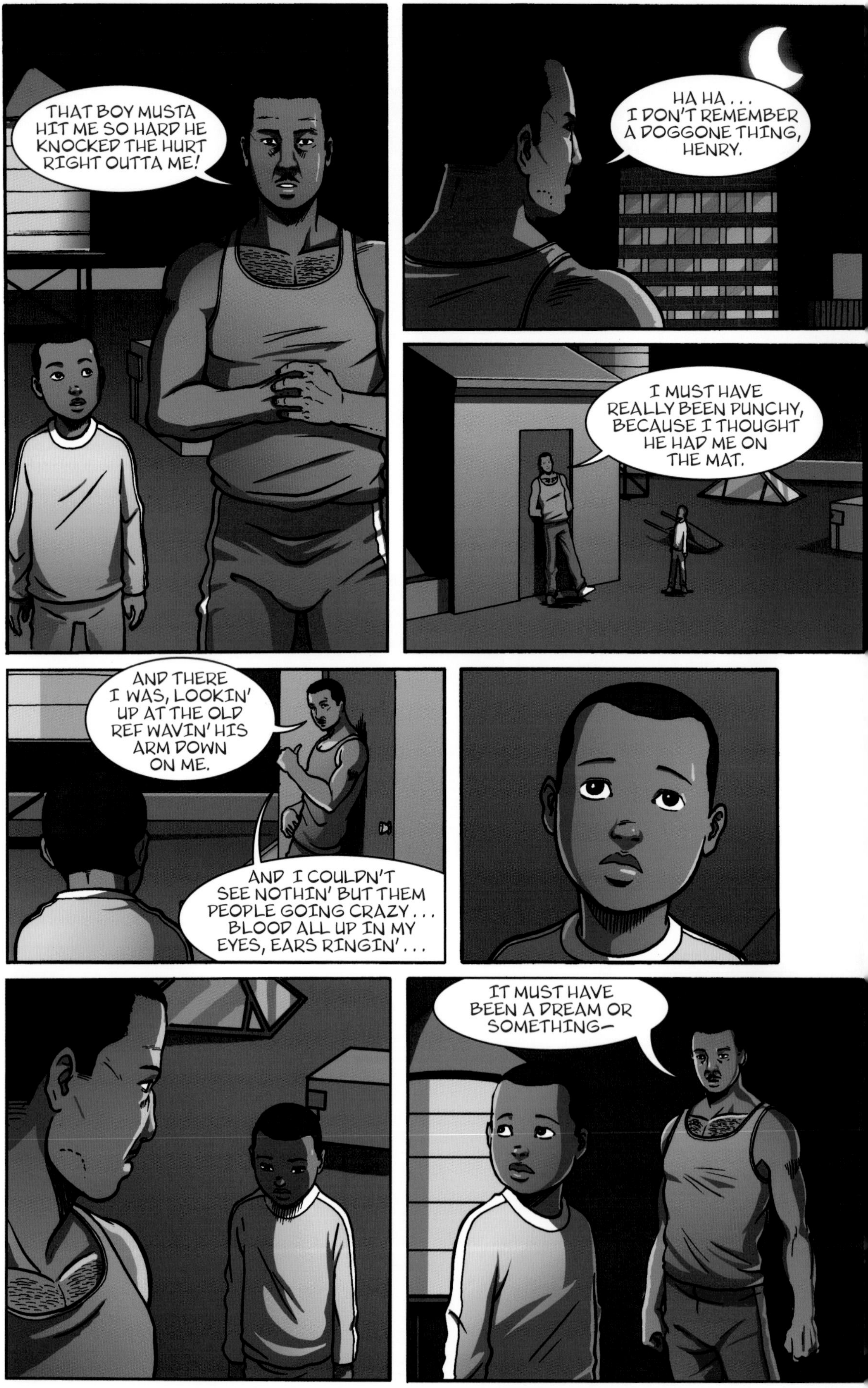
THAT BOY MUSTA HIT ME SO HARD HE KNOCKED THE HURT RIGHT OUTTA ME!
HA HA . . . I DON'T REMEMBER A DOGGONE THING, HENRY.
I MUST HAVE REALLY BEEN PUNCHY, BECAUSE I THOUGHT HE HAD ME ON THE MAT.
AND THERE I WAS, LOOKIN' UP AT THE OLD REF WAVIN' HIS ARM DOWN ON ME.
AND I COULDN'T SEE NOTHIN' BUT THEM PEOPLE GOING CRAZY . . . BLOOD ALL UP IN MY EYES, EARS RINGIN' . . .
IT MUST HAVE BEEN A DREAM OR SOMETHING—

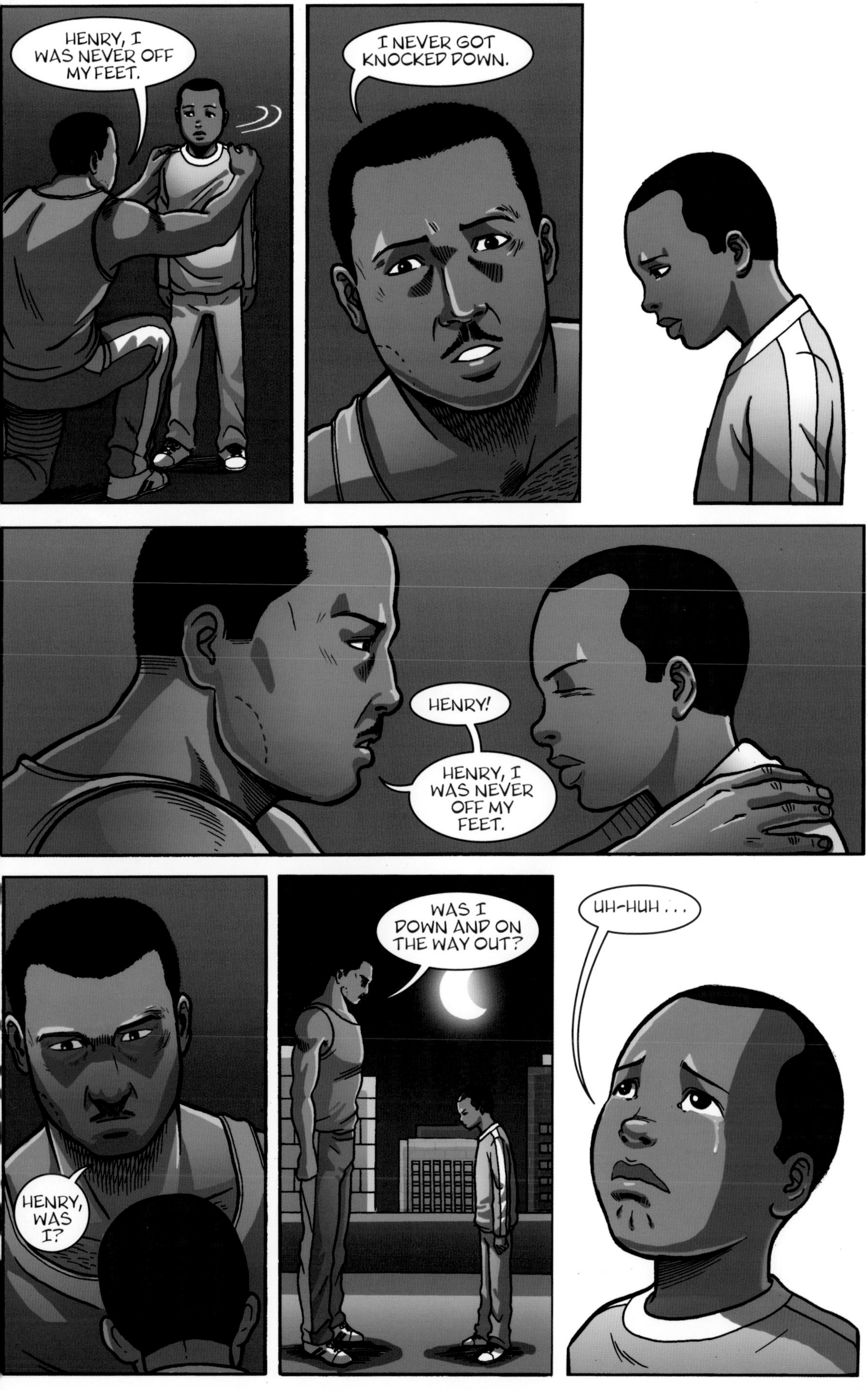
HENRY, I WAS NEVER OFF MY FEET.
I NEVER GOT KNOCKED DOWN.
HENRY!
HENRY, I WAS NEVER OFF MY FEET.
HENRY, WAS I?
WAS I DOWN AND ON THE WAY OUT?
UH-HUH . . .

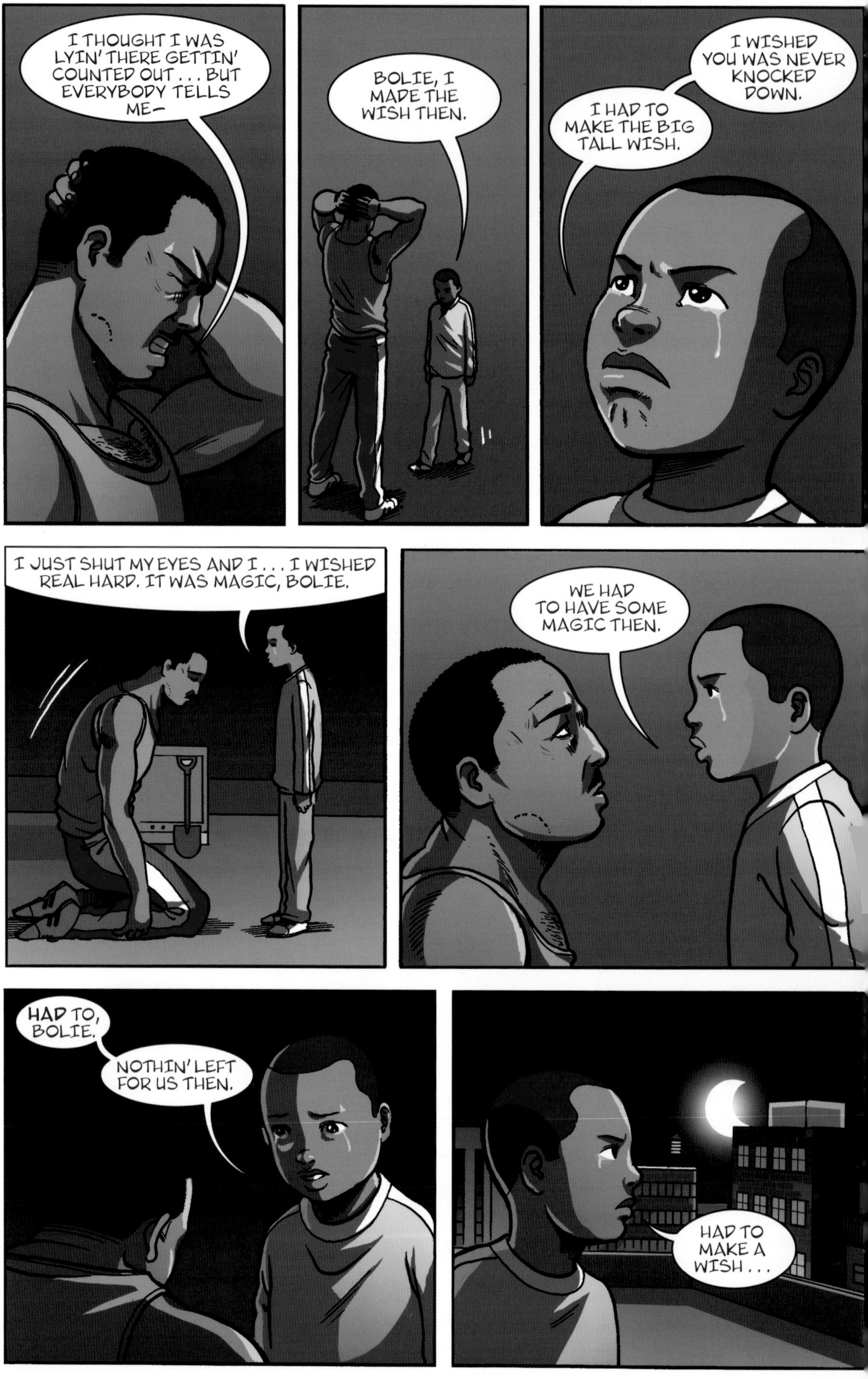
I THOUGHT I WAS LYIN' THERE GETTIN' COUNTED OUT . . . BUT EVERYBODY TELLS ME—
BOLIE, I MADE THE WISH THEN.
I WISHED YOU WAS NEVER KNOCKED DOWN.
I HAD TO MAKE THE BIG TALL WISH.
I JUST SHUT MY EYES AND I . . . I WISHED REAL HARD. IT WAS MAGIC, BOLIE.
WE HAD TO HAVE SOME MAGIC THEN.
HAD TO, BOLIE.
NOTHIN' LEFT FOR US THEN.
HAD TO MAKE A WISH . . .

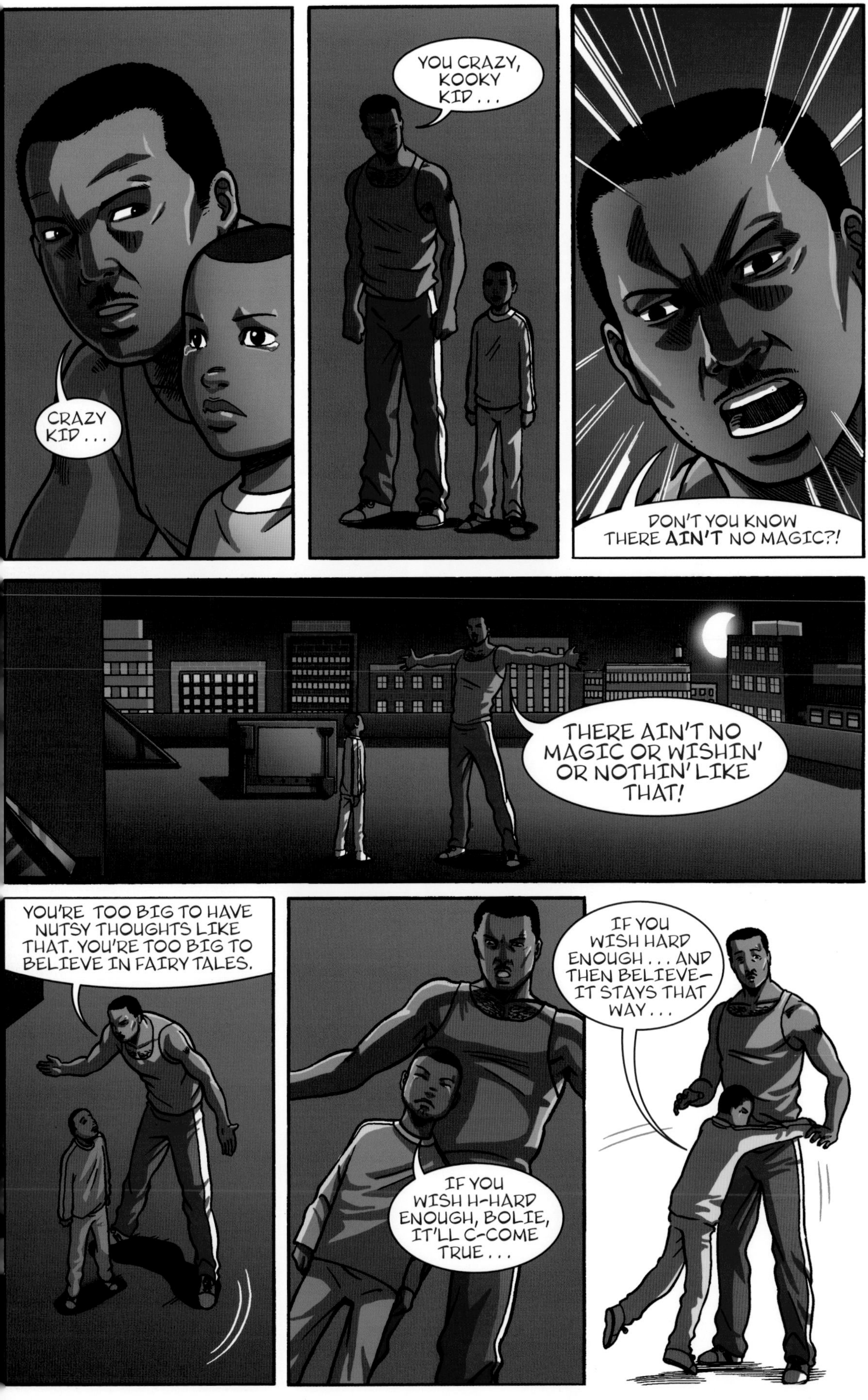
CRAZY KID . . .
YOU CRAZY, KOOKY KID . . .
DON'T YOU KNOW THERE **AIN'T** NO MAGIC?!
THERE AIN'T NO MAGIC OR WISHIN' OR NOTHIN' LIKE THAT!
YOU'RE TOO BIG TO HAVE NUTSY THOUGHTS LIKE THAT. YOU'RE TOO BIG TO BELIEVE IN FAIRY TALES.
IF YOU WISH H-HARD ENOUGH, BOLIE, IT'LL C-COME TRUE . . .
IF YOU WISH HARD ENOUGH . . . AND THEN BELIEVE— IT STAYS THAT WAY . . .

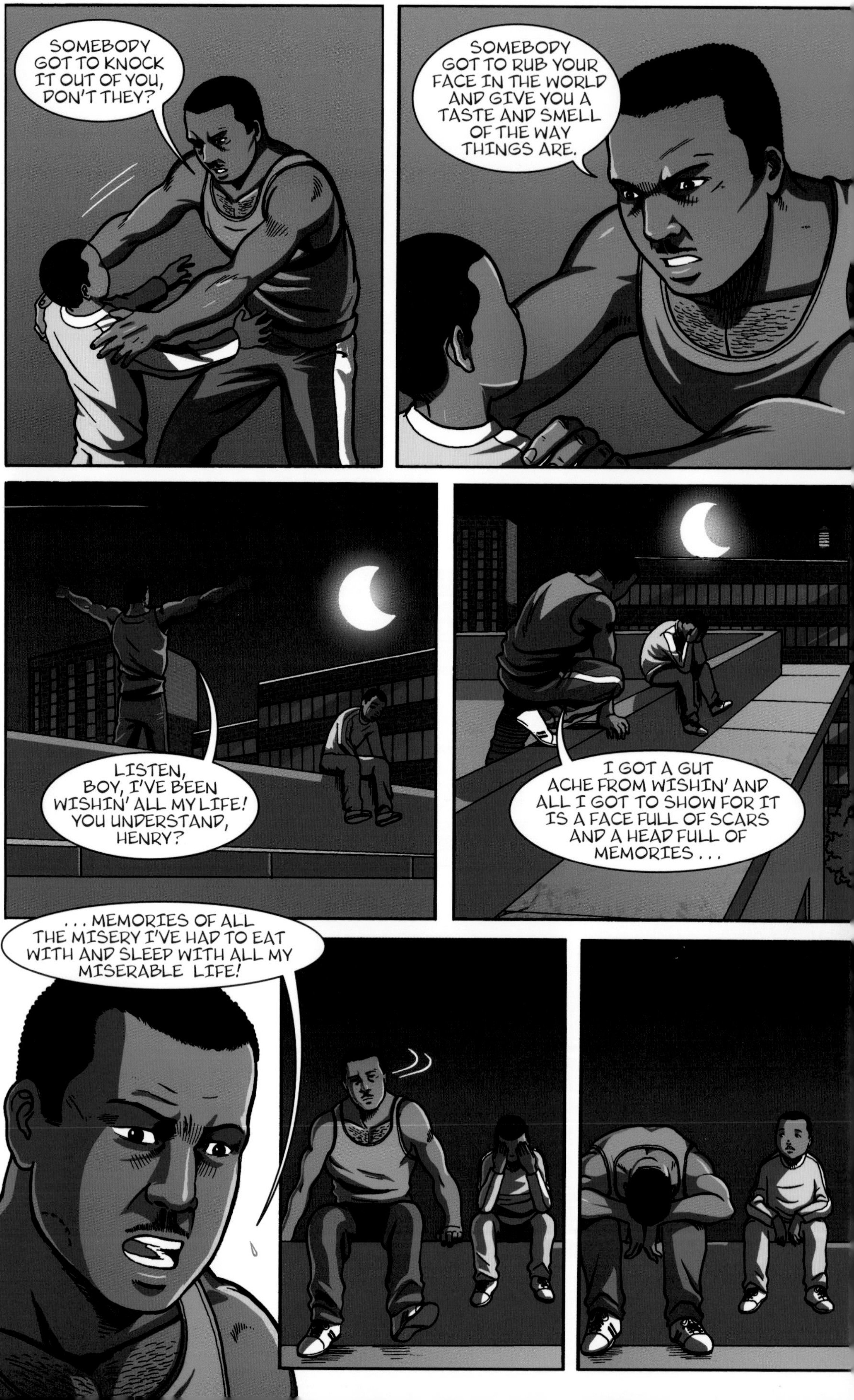
SOMEBODY GOT TO KNOCK IT OUT OF YOU, DON'T THEY?
SOMEBODY GOT TO RUB YOUR FACE IN THE WORLD AND GIVE YOU A TASTE AND SMELL OF THE WAY THINGS ARE.
LISTEN, BOY, I'VE BEEN WISHIN' ALL MY LIFE! YOU UNDERSTAND, HENRY?
I GOT A GUT ACHE FROM WISHIN' AND ALL I GOT TO SHOW FOR IT IS A FACE FULL OF SCARS AND A HEAD FULL OF MEMORIES . . .
. . . MEMORIES OF ALL THE MISERY I'VE HAD TO EAT WITH AND SLEEP WITH ALL MY MISERABLE LIFE!

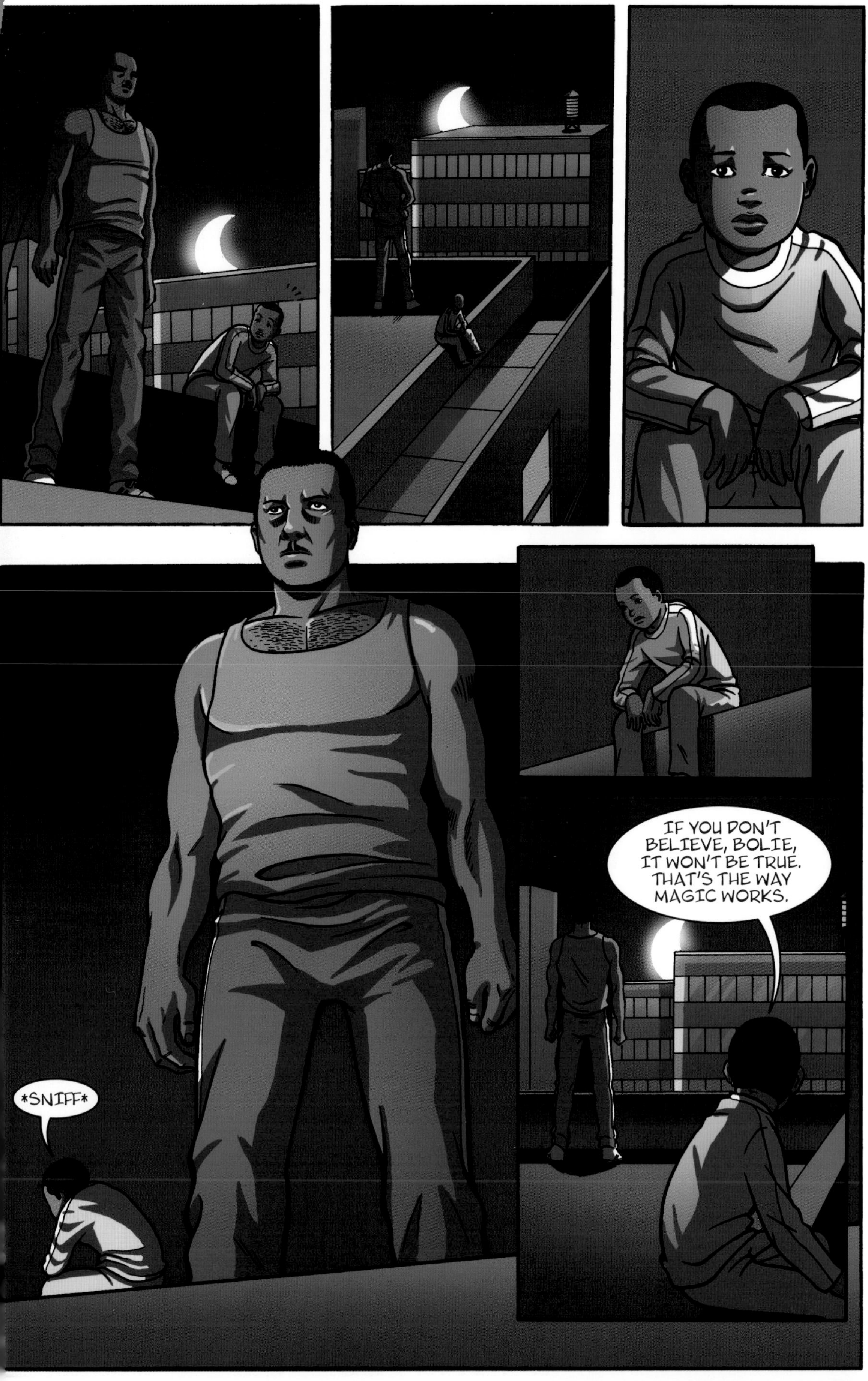
SNIFF
IF YOU DON'T BELIEVE, BOLIE, IT WON'T BE TRUE. THAT'S THE WAY MAGIC WORKS.

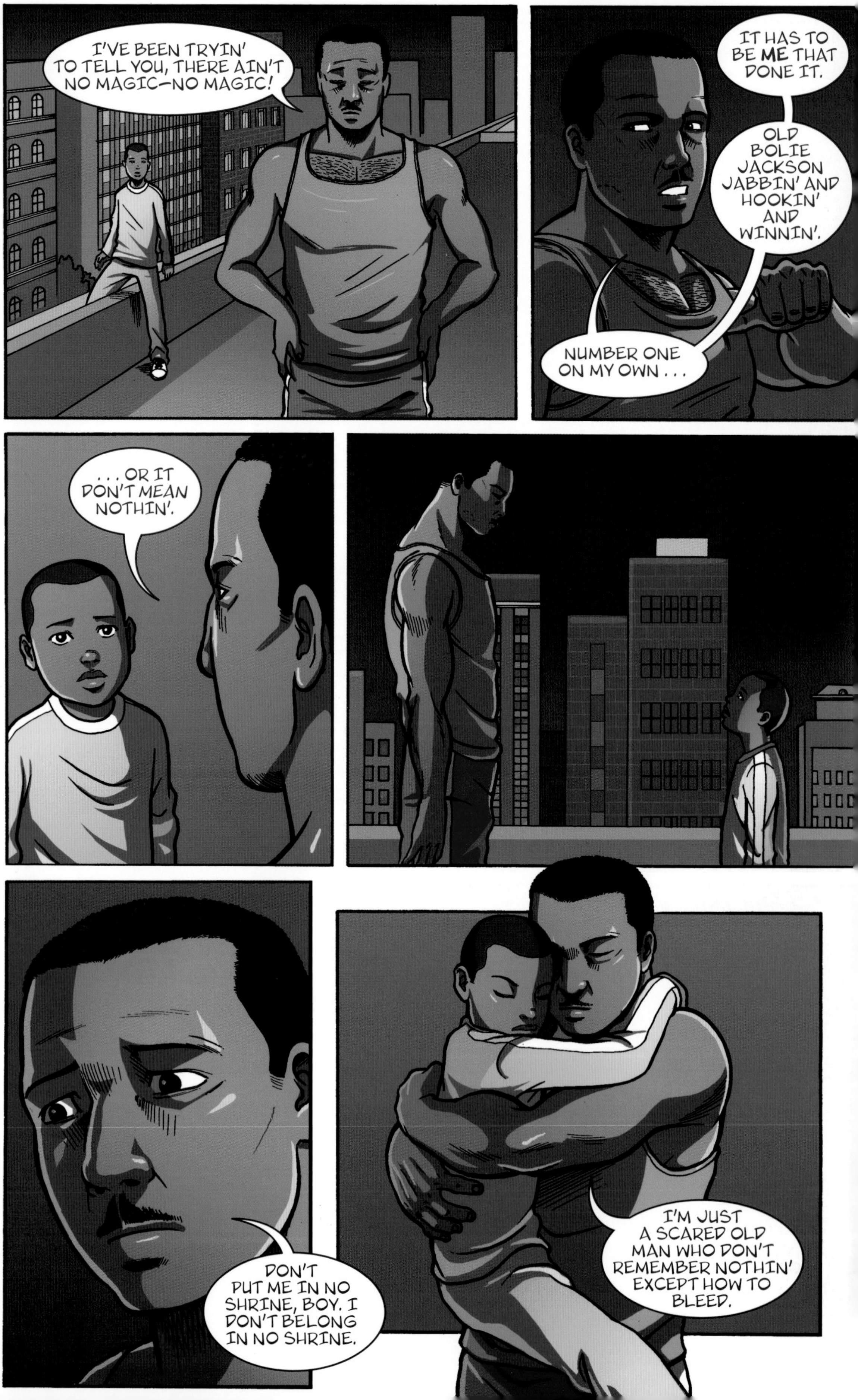
I'VE BEEN TRYIN' TO TELL YOU, THERE AIN'T NO MAGIC—NO MAGIC!
IT HAS TO BE ME THAT DONE IT.
OLD BOLIE JACKSON JABBIN' AND HOOKIN' AND WINNIN'.
NUMBER ONE ON MY OWN . . .
. . . OR IT DON'T MEAN NOTHIN'.
DON'T PUT ME IN NO SHRINE, BOY. I DON'T BELONG IN NO SHRINE.
I'M JUST A SCARED OLD MAN WHO DON'T REMEMBER NOTHIN' EXCEPT HOW TO BLEED.

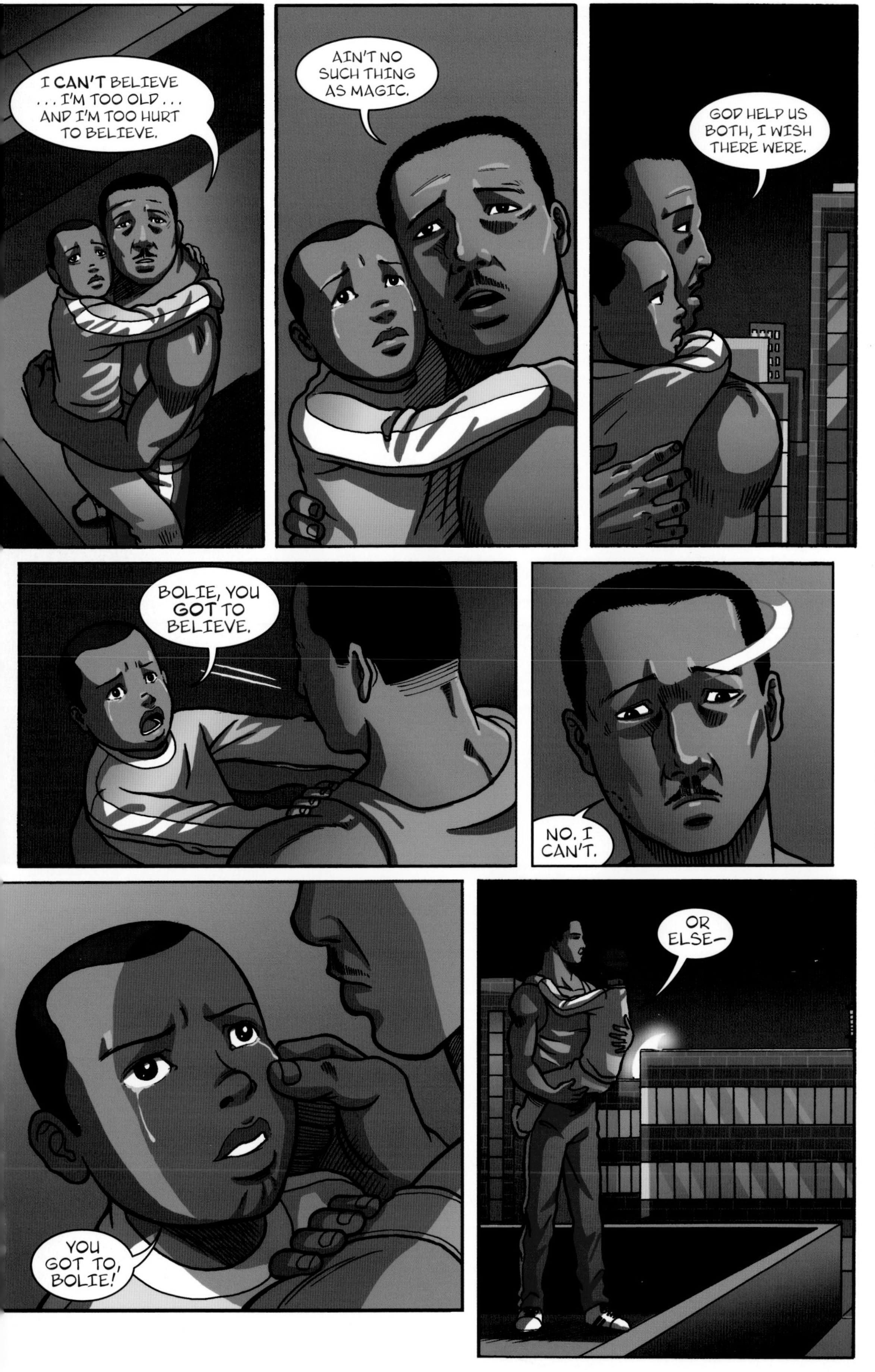
I CAN'T BELIEVE . . . I'M TOO OLD . . . AND I'M TOO HURT TO BELIEVE.
AIN'T NO SUCH THING AS MAGIC.
GOD HELP US BOTH, I WISH THERE WERE.
BOLIE, YOU GOT TO BELIEVE.
NO. I CAN'T.
YOU GOT TO, BOLIE!
OR ELSE—

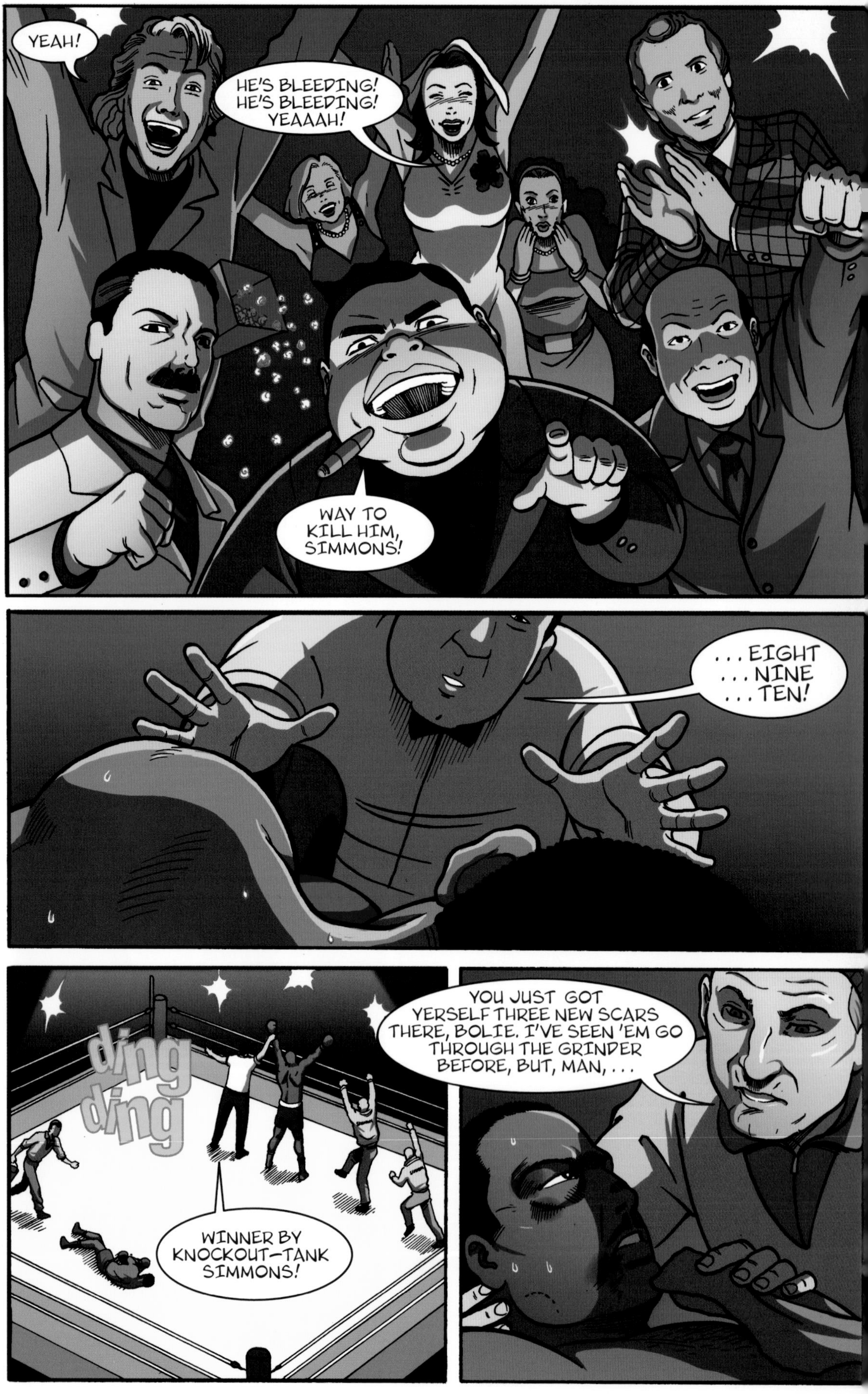
YEAH!
HE'S BLEEDING! HE'S BLEEDING! YEAAAH!
WAY TO KILL HIM, SIMMONS!
. . . EIGHT . . . NINE . . . TEN!
ding ding
WINNER BY KNOCKOUT—TANK SIMMONS!
YOU JUST GOT YERSELF THREE NEW SCARS THERE, BOLIE. I'VE SEEN 'EM GO THROUGH THE GRINDER BEFORE, BUT, MAN, . . .

WHAT YOU TRYIN' TO PROVE ANYWAY, OLD-TIMER?

. . . WHY'N'T YOU LET ME END THIS FIGHT LAST ROUND?

EVEN WITH TWO GOOD HANDS, THAT KID'S TWICE AS YOUNG AND TEN TIMES AS FAST AS YOU. . . . YOU NEVER HAD A CHANCE.

NOT SO FULL OF VINEGAR NOW, HUH, BOLIE?

WHAT ARE YOU DOIN' HERE, THOMAS?

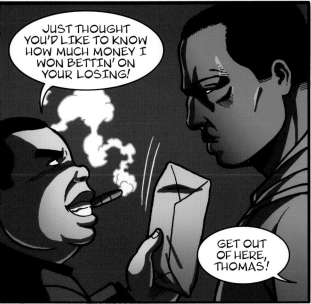

JUST THOUGHT YOU'D LIKE TO KNOW HOW MUCH MONEY I WON BETTIN' ON YOUR LOSING!

GET OUT OF HERE, THOMAS!

MAYBE NOW YOU WANNA THINK ABOUT SIGNIN' UP AT THE BACK DOOR, GETTIN' IN THE STABLE, HUH, BOLIE? HA HA HA. HUH, BOLIE? HA HA HA!

I SAID GET OUT!

ROTTEN BUZZARD!

HA HA HA HA

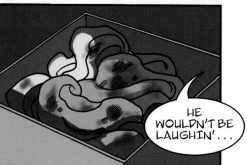

HE WOULDN'T BE LAUGHIN'...

...IF YOU'DA CONNECTED BEFORE.

NO SIRREE, HE'D STILL BE TRYIN' TO PULL HIS HEAD OUTTA THAT WALL.

BOLIE JACKSON VS TANK SIMMONS

KID DOVE VS BOB PENDARVER

ST. NICHO BOXING TON

YEP, THAT'S WHAT HE'D BE DOIN' ALL RIGHT...

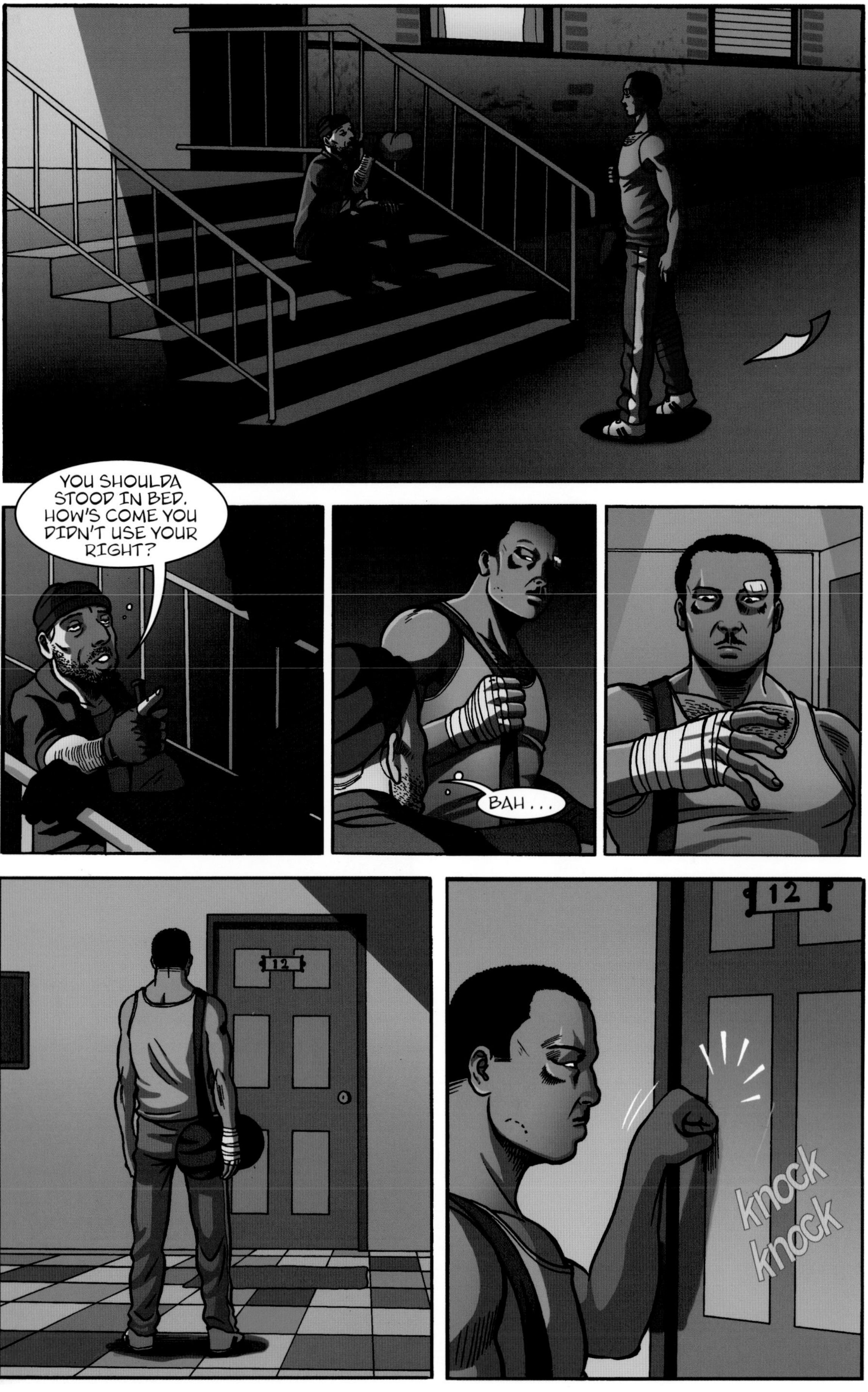
YOU SHOULDA STOOD IN BED. HOW'S COME YOU DIDN'T USE YOUR RIGHT?
BAH . . .
12
12
knock knock

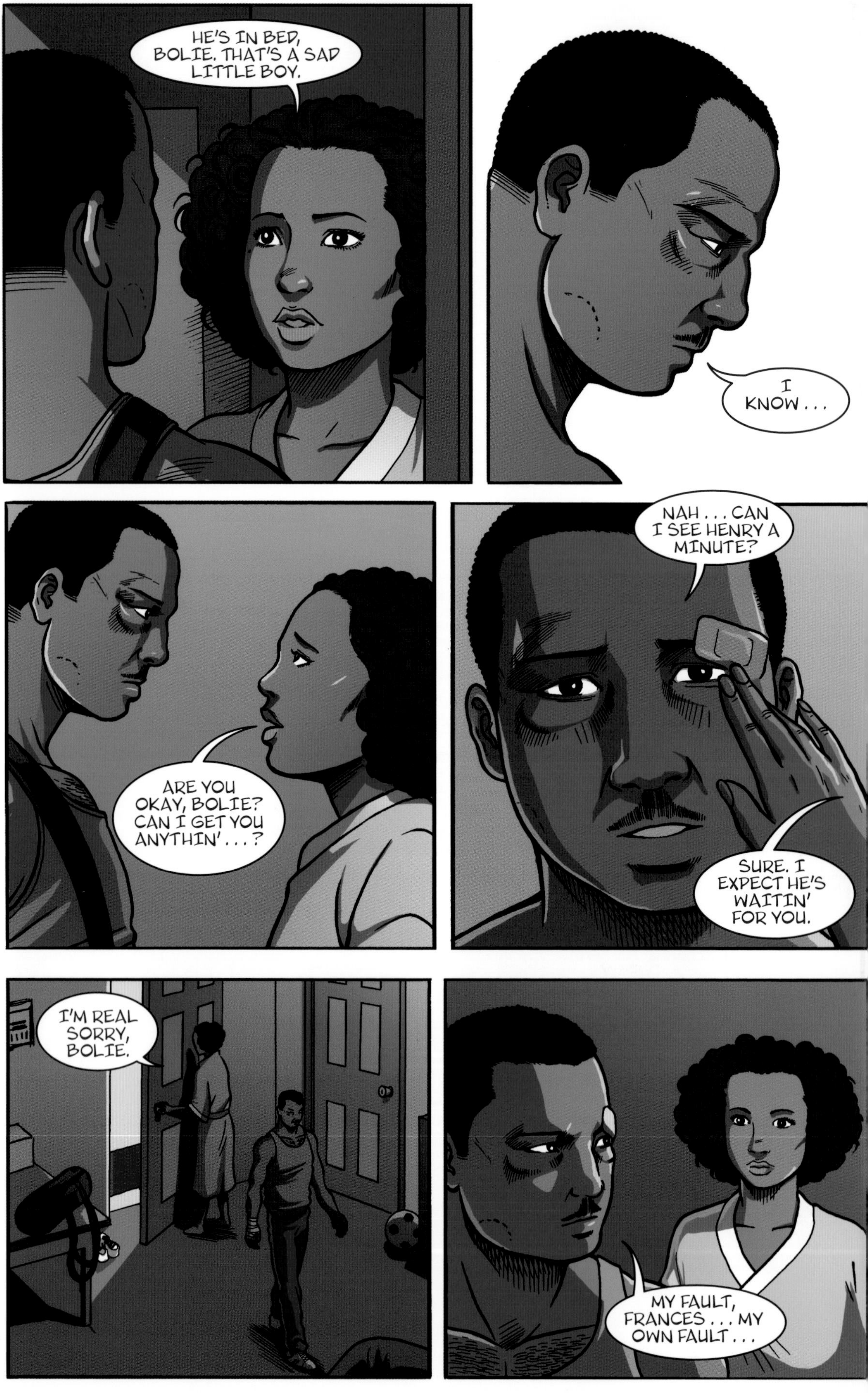
HE'S IN BED, BOLIE. THAT'S A SAD LITTLE BOY.
I KNOW . . .
ARE YOU OKAY, BOLIE? CAN I GET YOU ANYTHIN' . . . ?
NAH . . . CAN I SEE HENRY A MINUTE?
SURE. I EXPECT HE'S WAITIN' FOR YOU.
I'M REAL SORRY, BOLIE.
MY FAULT, FRANCES . . . MY OWN FAULT . . .

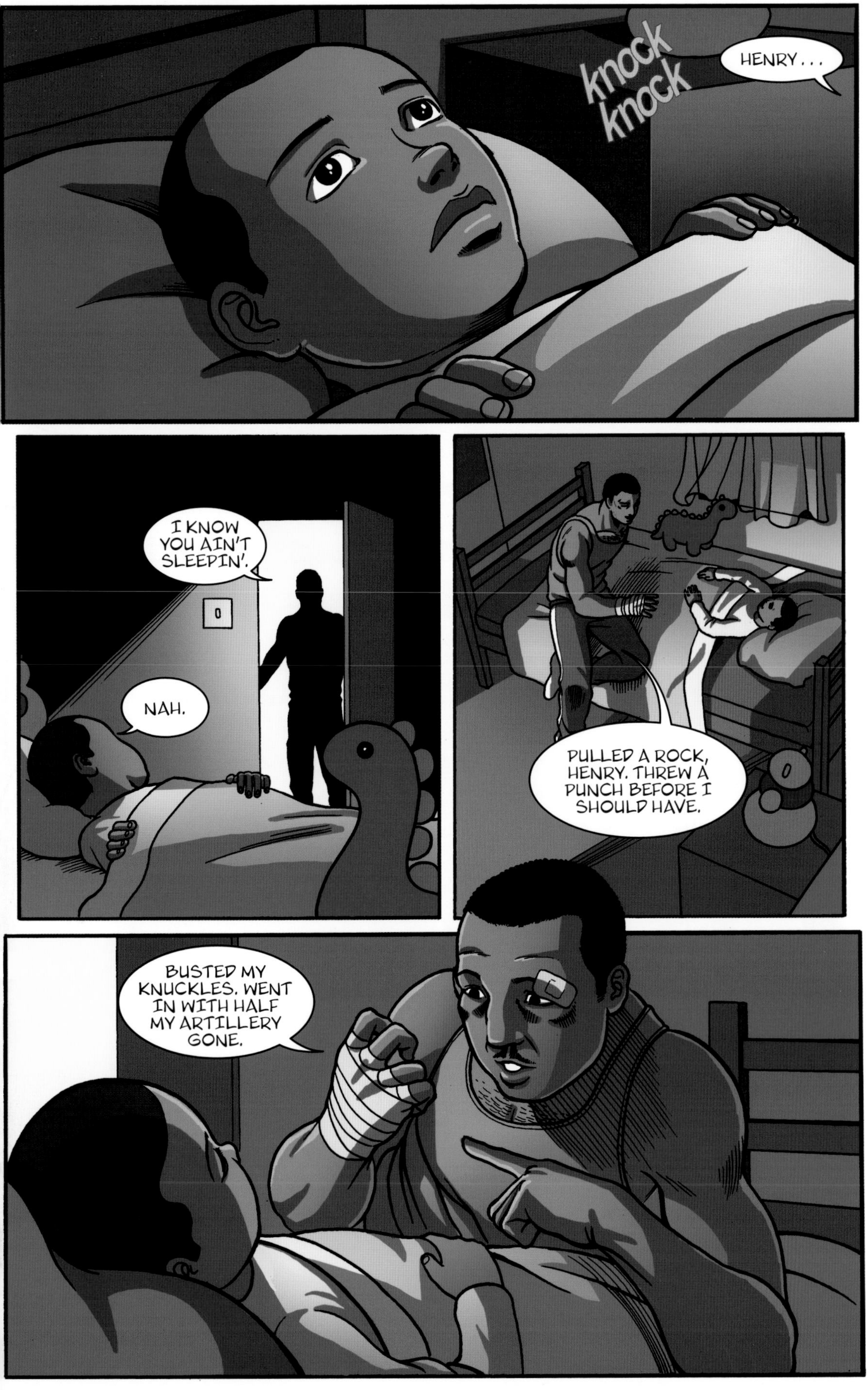
knock knock
HENRY . . .
I KNOW YOU AIN'T SLEEPIN'.
NAH.
PULLED A ROCK, HENRY. THREW A PUNCH BEFORE I SHOULD HAVE.
BUSTED MY KNUCKLES. WENT IN WITH HALF MY ARTILLERY GONE.

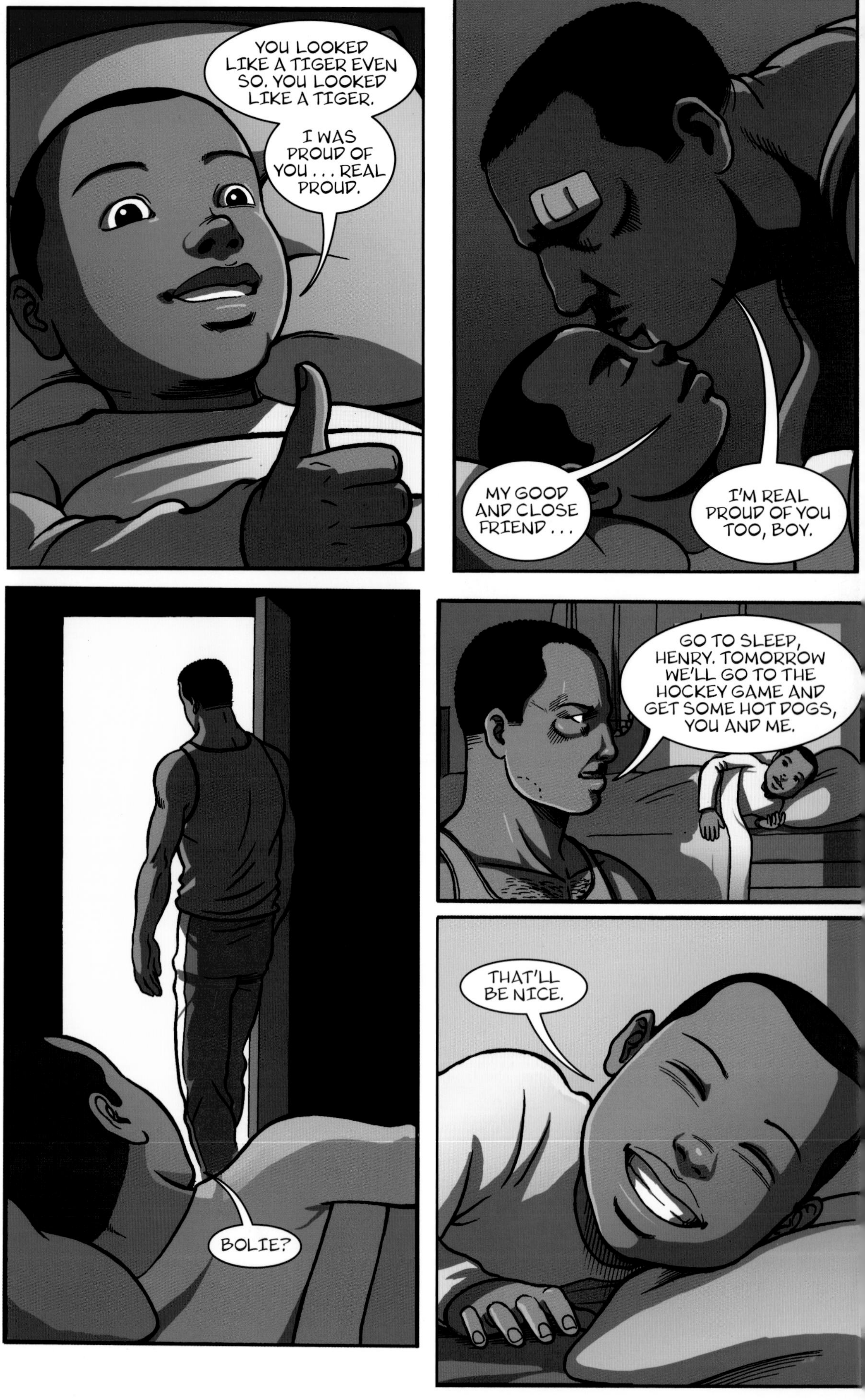
YOU LOOKED LIKE A TIGER EVEN SO. YOU LOOKED LIKE A TIGER.
I WAS PROUD OF YOU . . . REAL PROUD.
MY GOOD AND CLOSE FRIEND . . .
I'M REAL PROUD OF YOU TOO, BOY.
GO TO SLEEP, HENRY. TOMORROW WE'LL GO TO THE HOCKEY GAME AND GET SOME HOT DOGS, YOU AND ME.
THAT'LL BE NICE.
BOLIE?

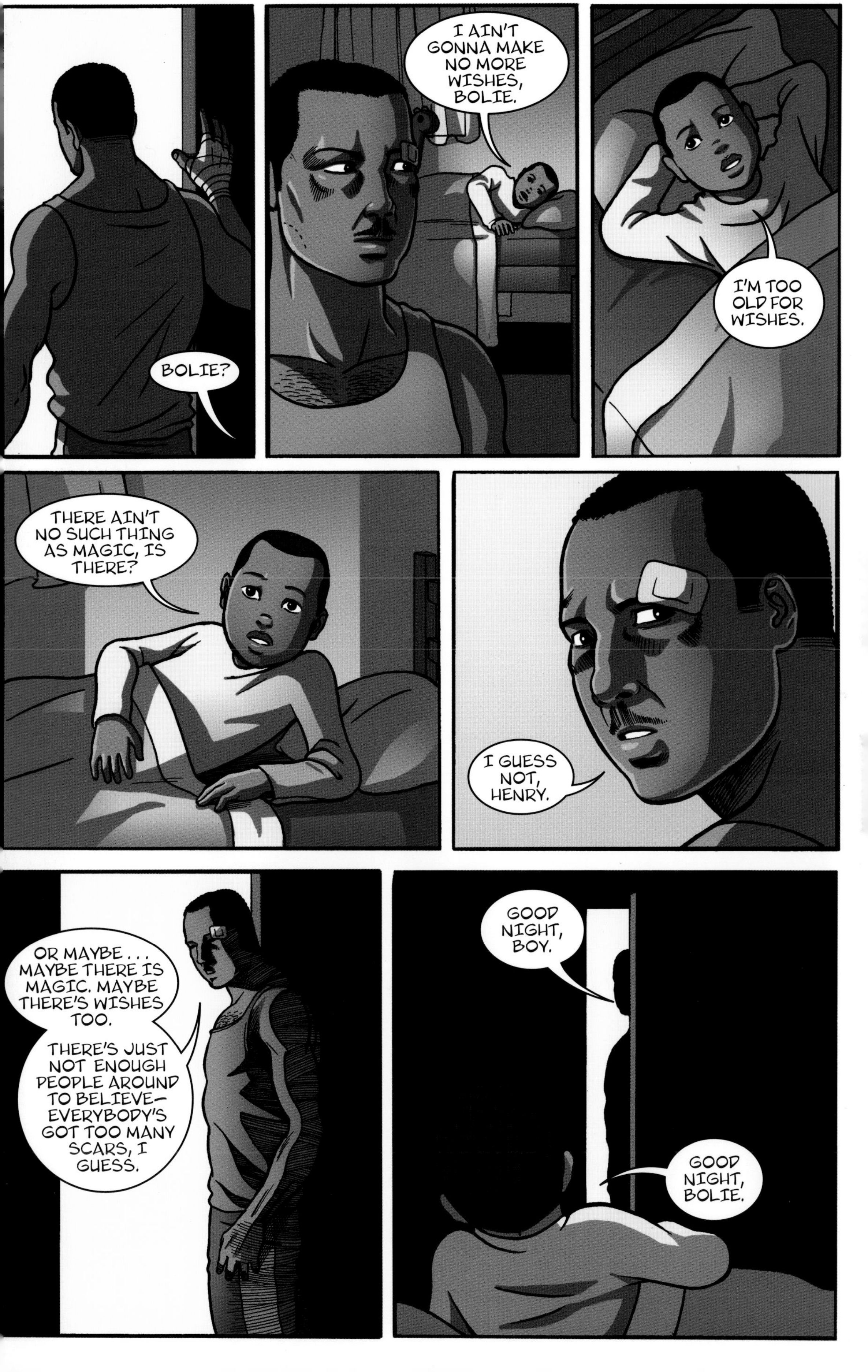
BOLIE?
I AIN'T GONNA MAKE NO MORE WISHES, BOLIE.
I'M TOO OLD FOR WISHES.
THERE AIN'T NO SUCH THING AS MAGIC, IS THERE?
I GUESS NOT, HENRY.
OR MAYBE . . . MAYBE THERE IS MAGIC. MAYBE THERE'S WISHES TOO.
THERE'S JUST NOT ENOUGH PEOPLE AROUND TO BELIEVE— EVERYBODY'S GOT TOO MANY SCARS, I GUESS.
GOOD NIGHT, BOY.
GOOD NIGHT, BOLIE.

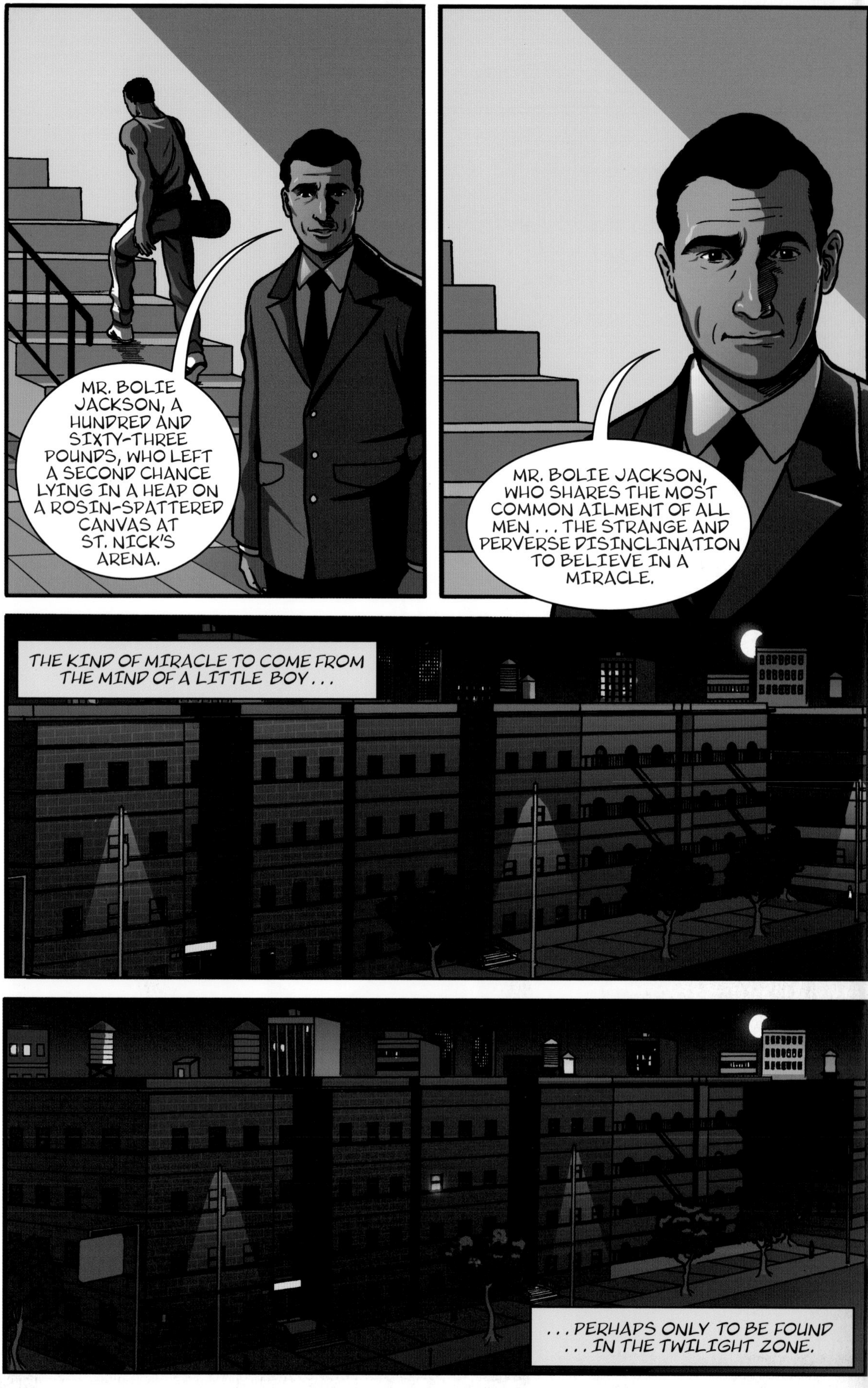
MR. BOLIE JACKSON, A HUNDRED AND SIXTY-THREE POUNDS, WHO LEFT A SECOND CHANCE LYING IN A HEAP ON A ROSIN-SPATTERED CANVAS AT ST. NICK'S ARENA.
MR. BOLIE JACKSON, WHO SHARES THE MOST COMMON AILMENT OF ALL MEN . . . THE STRANGE AND PERVERSE DISINCLINATION TO BELIEVE IN A MIRACLE.
THE KIND OF MIRACLE TO COME FROM THE MIND OF A LITTLE BOY . . .
. . . PERHAPS ONLY TO BE FOUND . . . IN THE TWILIGHT ZONE.

The Big Tall Wish

Season One, Episode #27

Original Air Date: April 8, 1960

Written by Rod Serling

Cast

Narrator: Rod Serling

Bolie Jackson: Ivan Dixon*
* Also appeared in *I Am the Night—Color Me Black* as Reverend Anderson

Henry: Stephen Perry (as Steven Perry)

Frances: Kim Hamilton

Joe Mizell: Walter Burke

Thomas: Henry Scott*
*Also appeared in *The Thirty-Fathom Grave* as Jr. OOD

Fighter: Charles Horvath (uncredited)

Announcer: Carl McIntire (uncredited)

Referee: Frankie Van (uncredited)

Crew

Producer: Buck Houghton
Director: Ron Winston
Director of Photography: George T. Clemens
Film Editor: Bill Mosher

Production Note

A television episode cast primarily with African American actors was a true rarity in 1960—especially for a story that was not about racial strife. In fact, it was so unusual that in 1961 *The Twilight Zone* was awarded the Unity Award for Outstanding Contributions to Better Race Relations for this episode and several others that also featured African American actors. Champion boxer Archie Moore was originally cast as Bolie but was replaced by Ivan Dixon, a well-respected stage actor who went on to achieve fame in the TV series *Hogan's Heroes.*

ADAPTING STORIES FROM ROD SERLING'S
THE TWILIGHT ZONE

In terms of screenwriting adaptations it's trying to cut out stuff that's extraneous, without doing damage to the original piece, because you owe a debt of some respect to the original author.

—Rod Serling, 1975

At first, the idea sounded straightforward. Take an original *Twilight Zone* screenplay and adapt it into a graphic novel—break the visuals into panels, move the dialogue into balloons and captions. After all, Rod Serling himself was a fan of comics, and graphic novels are their visual and literary heirs. Serling collected Entertaining Comics titles such as *Tales from the Crypt* and *Weird Science*, the themes of which resonate in *The Twilight Zone*; even Serling's trademark narration could be considered an echo of the Crypt Keeper's introductions. Yet the more I considered the task of adapting the scripts, the more the gravity of what I was doing set in. I grew up watching *The Twilight Zone*, after all, as did so many Americans. The work required a certain reverential perspective, considering the show's iconic status, not to mention the quality of the original material.

In the 1950s the comics Serling had enjoyed were considered subversive, a threat to America's youth. Frederick Wertham published *Seduction of the Innocent* in 1954, excoriating comics in an atmosphere of public paranoia similar to a scene from *The Monsters Are Due on Maple Street*. A year later, a Senate committee was convened to investigate the pernicious influence of horror comics on America's youth, and the Comics Code Authority was established to censor comics' content. EC Comics went out of business as a direct result. In an interesting twist of fate, by the end of the decade *The Twilight Zone* was just beginning to find its television audience with stories that probably would not have made it past the comics censors. Recreating Serling's stories now, in graphic novel form, seems appropriate, emblematic of an era in which comics are finding a new readership, achieving new respect, and speaking to a new audience receptive to a more sophisticated message.

Serling's stories run the gamut from serious drama, filled with fantastic and frightening dilemmas of the human condition, to wry, tongue-in-cheek humor in a sci-fi wrapper. Selecting eight as graphic novel material meant making difficult choices. Serling was a prolific writer, creating more than half of *The Twilight Zone's* 156 scripts. It was not only a question of which of these would work best in novelized format, but which ones, as a group, would come closest to capturing the essence of *The Twilight Zone*. The stories ultimately chosen for these books possess the strongest visual possibilities and reflect an effort to achieve a cross section of Serling's dramatic range.

As I began adapting the stories for artists, I immersed myself in the screenplays and watched each episode until I felt I had internalized not just the characters, the plot, and the point, but what I imagined to be something of the author himself. In the process, I felt a growing kinship with Serling. Parts of the screenplay were often deleted from the actual show. Lines, characters, even entire scenes were struck, sometimes for budgetary reasons, sometimes because of time constraints, sometimes perhaps because Serling himself may have anticipated problems with the scenes. The show usually had only a thirty-minute time slot. The deleted scenes, however, often add richness and complexity to the story, offering a glimmer into what Serling might have done were it not for the constraints of the television medium. Restoring scenes seemed to help push the story even harder. I felt as if I were developing Serling's original design, following the telling to its logical conclusion.

With each of these stories, I have aspired to take advantage of what the graphic novel format can do. Art and text draw the reader deeply into the narrative. The reader does not just hear, but ponders, actively bridging the gaps between the panels of art with his or her own imagination. The story doesn't just happen to the reader, but, in part, *is* the reader. In other words, *The Twilight Zone* episodes had to be recreated not just to fit into a graphic novel format but to belong to it.

As much as possible, I have endeavored to keep the intentions of the original story intact—that is the "debt of respect" owed to Serling—fully functional in a new medium. From some nearby fifth dimension, I hope Serling is smiling at the prospect of these books, pleased at the thought of a new generation arriving by way of a different avenue perhaps, but entering and being welcomed into the fold of "Zonies" around the world.

—Mark Kneece
Professor of Sequential Art, Savannah College of Art and Design

Acknowledgments

Our thanks go to Carol Serling for her time and consideration while reviewing the adaptation texts and illustrated pages, and also to John Lowe, chair of the Sequential Art Department at Savannah College of Art and Design, for his assistance in pairing the right artists with the right stories.

First published in the United States of America in 2009 by Walker Publishing Company, Inc.
Visit Walker & Company's Web site at www.walkeryoungreaders.com
Visit the Savannah College of Art and Design's Web Site at www.scad.edu

For information about permission to reproduce selections from this book, write to
Permissions, Walker & Company, 175 Fifth Avenue, New York, New York 10010

Library of Congress Cataloging-in-Publication Data
Kneece, Mark.
The twilight zone : the big tall wish / by Rod Serling ; adapted by Mark Kneece ; illustrated by Chris Lie.
p.   cm.
Summary: A washed-up boxer who is about to lose a fight suddenly finds himself switching places with his opponent based on the wish of a young friend.
ISBN-13: 978-0-8027-9724-7 • ISBN-10: 0-8027-9724-5 (hardcover)
ISBN-13: 978-0-8027-9725-4 • ISBN-10: 0-8027-9725-3 (paperback)
1. Graphic novels. [1. Graphic novels. 2. Boxing—Fiction. 3. Magic—Fiction. 4. African Americans—Fiction.]
I. Serling, Rod, 1924–1975. II. Lie, Chris, ill. III. Twilight zone (Television program : 1959–1964) IV. Title. V. Title: Big tall wish.
PZ7.7.K65Twd 2009   [Fic]—dc22   2008043812

Packaged by Design Press, a division of Savannah College of Art and Design, Inc.˙
22 East Lathrop Street, Savannah, Georgia 31415

Adaptation from Rod Serling's original script by Mark Kneece
Illustrated by Chris Lie and Caravan Studio
Lettering by Thomas Zielonka
Series title treatment by Devin O'Bryan
Series copyediting by Kerri O'Hern
Series creative development by Anna Marlis Burgard and Emily Easton
Series art direction and design by Angela Rojas
Series project management by Angela Rojas and Melissa Kavonic
Creative consultant: Carol Serling

Photograph of Rod Serling © Bettmann/Corbis

Printed in China
2 4 6 8 10 9 7 5 3 1 (hardcover)
2 4 6 8 10 9 7 5 3 1 (paperback)

All papers used by Walker & Company are natural, recyclable products
made from wood grown in well-managed forests. The manufacturing processes
conform to the environmental regulations of the country of origin.